Ravenwood:
Volume Two

Imprint: Imagine Nation

Imagine Nation

Chenoa, IL 61726

AuthorJenniferLush@gmail.com

Chapter One

Litmus Test

'*I can't believe you're still scared of a ghost story.*'

This weekend was much needed, and the semester had barely started. Ever since returning from her visit home over the summer, Colby had been on her back constantly about a picture she was tagged in by a friend on social media. A group of friends had a get together shortly before she returned to Boston for fall classes, and of course, they took a picture together. Many of these faces she may never see again.

There were already a handful from her old group who weren't there. A couple went back to college early. One didn't come home for the summer. The rest had drifted away after high school ended. People's lives go on separate paths. It happens unfortunately.

Try telling that to Colby. If you ask him, Liv had slept with half her home town while texting him every night saying how much she missed him. When the picture posted two days before she went back to campus, he asked her about it. Nothing more. It wasn't until they were face to face again when the accusations started. "Who are those guys? How do you know them? What were you doing with them? You seemed pretty friendly in the photo."

Liv had been friends with them since kindergarten. The

thought of being anything more than friends with them disgusted her. That's not what their relationship was about and never would be.

'You know it's not real, right?'

It had been constant for the first couple of days. The picture preoccupied Colby's every waking moment. It had died down in the last couple weeks, but it was still mentioned daily.

As bad as that was, her friends had to chime in their own two cents about it. They believed he was deflecting. He had stepped out of line over the summer and cheated on her. This picture was his opportunity to throw everything onto her, so she wouldn't figure it out.

It was so confusing. Liv didn't know what to think anymore. It needed to stop. She was tired of hearing about it. She was fed up with him trying to make her feel guilty over having a fun night with friends. If it didn't end soon, like now, it was going to be over between them. This weekend was her gauge for that decision. It was a test to see if anything felt different between them and whether or not he could let the subject drop. So far, things were going smoothly, but it had only been one night.

'Liv's a scaredy-cat! Look at her! She believes it.'

When the car began to slow down, Liv woke up. She hadn't meant to doze off and hoped she hadn't been out long. She peered over the back of the seats in front of her to see out the windshield. They were in the middle of nowhere in an area she didn't recognize. They had stopped for the night not far past Barre and were going to drive around the western part of the state for a while today before making their way back to Boston for classes on Tuesday. Depending on how long she had been out, they could be anywhere.

"Where are we? What are we doing?"

"We've been in the car for so long. Thought we could stretch our legs," Logan told her. "Besides, I need to take a leak." He pulled the car off onto the shoulder.

There was nothing specific which told her where they were. It was a two lane road in the middle of a beautiful country side. There was an open meadow on one side and nothing but trees on the other.

"Where are we?" she asked again. Her voice cracked a little this time from the fear and panic swelling in her chest.

Logan continued getting out of the car with Colby right behind him. Kylie sat in the front seat giggling.

'These idiots.' Liv looked around outside the car to see where the guys had gone. *'They brought us to Ravenwood.'* She had never taken the risk of driving Route 116 to recognize anything, and there were no road markers in sight to prove it. The feeling of dread settled over her like a musty death shroud, and it was all the evidence she needed.

'Liv won't go camping. She's afraid of nature.'

Freshman year is when they met. Anatomy and physiology was one of the hardest classes she had taken, and the four of them decided to form a study group. They studied hard during these meet ups. She'd barely have passed the class without them. By the end of the night, their books would be closed, and they'd hang out for hours. They became really close and eventually one thing led to another with Colby.

One night, they were sharing stories about their hometowns. Kylie's from California which was like a whole different world to Liv compared to where she grew up in western Massachusetts. Logan told them about the Waverly Hills Sanitorium in Kentucky near where he grew up. He painted a horrific picture about a tuberculosis outbreak and how this place was always over capacity and secretly removed the dead bodies. It was supposed to be haunted now. A number of people had investigated it, and anyone could pay to tour it. It was the spookiest place in America the way Logan told it.

"I've been there," he said. "It felt like something was following me, trying to almost push me to leave. I'll never go back."

The other two seemed interested in it. They believed in spirits. That's why Liv felt like they would enjoy hearing about Ravenwood as well. She was from the southern part of the state, closer to Westfield, but the tales of Ravenwood had made their way to her. Every story she heard about those woods or the castle made her think it couldn't get worse, but the next one always seemed to top it somehow.

"Yeah, right," Kylie laughed.

Colby teased her for days saying she couldn't tell a ghost story to save her life.

"You can't expect us to believe a tree is capable of action like that," Logan shook his head. "That's a crock right there."

'This one thinks trees are the judges of us in the end.'

They have made fun of her ever since. The first couple weeks they were nonstop ripping into her over it. They spoke to her in sing song baby voices whenever a tree was nearby asking if she was afraid for her life. One of them found a way to work it in to almost every conversation, even the study groups. "I bet the trees in Ravenwood know the cuneiform bones. They'd have to with all the torturing they do." Whenever one made a joke, the other two would laugh until they cried.

Eventually, it died down, but it never completely stopped. They could go a month or more without mentioning Ravenwood then out of nowhere came another snide remark. Liv regretted saying anything, but she wasn't about to take them out there to prove it either.

She heard Logan talking outside the car, and it yanked her back to reality harshly. "I heard there's a castle somewhere out in these woods. Thought it'd be fun to investigate it," he said to Colby.

"Oh, no," she mumbled from the back seat.

"What's the matter?" Kylie asked.

Liv had forgot she was still in the car. "We're in Ravenwood, aren't we?" she asked quietly. It wasn't a question which needed to be answered, but for some reason, she needed to hear someone say it.

"Really, Liv," Kylie said, opening her door. "It's not that big of a deal."

Just breathe.' She watched Kylie walk over to the guys and say something too quiet for her to hear. They laughed, and all of them looked at her. *'This can't be happening. They did not bring me to Ravenwood.'*

Colby was motioning for her to get out of the car, but she didn't move a muscle. The road didn't scare her. She could stand on the road, but if she stepped out of the car, it would be harder for her to convince them to get back in it.

He opened the rear door on the driver's side and leaned in to her. "C'mon, Liv. Get out."

"No," she shook her head.

"The car is off. It's going to get hot in here real fast. Stop being a baby." Colby slammed the door shut.

Hearing the word baby, the other two mimicked a cry and bawled their hands into fists pretending to rub their eyes. '*Why am I friends with them again?*' Liv understood what they were doing and wasn't really mad at them for it. She'd probably do the same thing at Waverly Hills Sanitorium if she was with someone who was scared to go inside. They were the ones who didn't understand. Her stories were real, and they were putting everyone's lives on the line.

They weren't going to stop. They'd leave her in the car and march into the woods making fun of her the whole way. Her only hope of stopping them was talking to them which would be easier if she joined them.

'*They're trees, Liv. They are incapable of harming anything or anyone intentionally.*'

"About time," Colby snapped.

Kylie grinned at her. "Logan said there's a castle in the woods."

'*Oh, yeah?*' Liv rolled her eyes. '*Wonder who told him about that?*'

"We're going to go find it," Kylie added.

"If you want to see the Ravenwood Inn, just go down to the lane and drive up to it."

"We can hike through from here." Logan was studying the tree line like he was looking for the best spot to enter. The ditch on the woods side of the road hadn't been mowed in ages. It couldn't be easy finding someone willing to do the work in these parts.

Liv stepped back away from the car, away from the trees. She walked backward until she was on the other side of the road. "I'm not going into the woods."

"I've been checking into this place," Colby said. "It's a litmus test. Only good people are allowed to leave."

'The trees can't hold someone hostage.'

The laughter came out of her mouth so fast it surprised herself. *'How many times did they tell me I was crazy for believing these stories? Now, he's acting like its real? Can't believe me though.'*

"The trees don't allow good people to leave. They allow people who are good to the trees to leave. There's a difference." Although she often wondered how big a difference it was. Generally speaking, a decent person would respect nature anyway.

"It's amazing to me you can say that with a straight face," Colby sneered.

"What?"

Kylie had joined Logan, and they made it through the ditch and were standing right in front of the woods. It was like they had a heads up to give her and Colby some privacy.

"You have no problems acting goody-goody about Ravenwood and those ridiculous stories but can't keep your legs closed for two months over the summer."

It was her final straw. This jerk was going to use her fear of these trees as proof she had cheated on him. For the first time, she wished she had. Part of her wanted to cheat on him just to make the accusations true.

"Do what you want to do," she said. "I'm not going to be a part of it."

"Why are you afraid of going into the woods?" Colby asked loudly. "Is it because you messed around on me, and you're afraid of the woods casting judgment upon you?"

Liv crossed her arms and shot an angry look in Kylie's direction. She had been the loudest voice in her ear about Colby accusing her of what he actually did, but she left her to fend for herself against him. "First of all, I never cheated on you. Secondly, the woods wouldn't care. I'm afraid of tripping over a root, falling, breaking a branch on my way down, and having the trees shove their roots down my throat and out through my ribs because I injured it!"

'If the body count in that area was as high as you claim, everyone would have heard of this place by now.'

Everyone laughed at her. "Go on into the woods," she challenged them. "You'll see what I mean."

Colby ran over to the other two. "If you have nothing to hide, you'll join us," he yelled as he went.

Liv checked side to side not sure which direction led where. She figured they must have been traveling toward Appleton because if the car had slowed down to drive through the town, she probably would've woken up then. She grabbed her purse from the car, leaving her bag in the trunk and started walking. If she was going the wrong way, the longer route, she'd just have to walk farther.

She didn't care anymore. She didn't care if they went into the woods. She didn't care if they survived. She didn't care if they were eaten alive by a bush. She was done.

They hollered after her for the first couple minutes. Correction: Colby hollered out more accusations and insults. The other two said nothing she could hear. The shouts became more muffled which she thought was due to the distance between them, but then they changed completely. The sounds of them beating their way through the trees echoed through the woods. They were acting like fools and were going to learn the hard way. Soon, the three of them were feigning being attacked, yelling to her for help. She was so angry she hoped it was real.

Liv stopped in her tracks. *'No, I don't. I don't want anything to happen to them. I'm just mad.'*

She kept walking at a brisk pace until her side pained. It was a sharp reminder of how out of shape she was and her empty vows to use the free gym on campus. She stopped and looked back but couldn't see anything. The car wasn't even in view. The road had a few turns in it as she walked, so she hoped that's why she couldn't see it. She didn't think Logan would drive off with the others and strand her in the middle of the country if they got back in the car and left when she didn't go with them.

'You put maple syrup on your pancakes? Aren't you afraid the trees will retaliate over their missing sap?'

Not long after that, she heard a car coming down the road behind her. Liv turned around and saw Logan's car. The car stopped when she did, and stayed in the middle of the road, revving the engine. She couldn't see anyone in the car, but there was a glare on the windshield preventing her from seeing who was driving. Her immediate thought was two of them had lost their lives to Ravenwood.

With her luck, it was Colby driving, and he was now blaming her for their friends' deaths. She kept walking, wondering where she'd run if he tried to hit her. Going into the trees was out of the question. On the other side of the road was an open meadow with a barbed wire fence. She wouldn't make it over before the car reached her.

The car finally made its way to her and pulled up alongside. Liv snuck a peek sideways without moving her head. There was no one in the car. It was driving on its own.

Liv panicked and increased her pace. She had heard stories of people who were attacked on the road, but those stories were so rare. It made her doubt them thinking the story had changed so much through retellings, and it probably actually occurred in the woods. Some might be made up completely. She'd never doubt those stories again if she lived to hear any more.

The car pulled up next to her again, but this time she heard a woman's voice. "Do you want a ride?"

Liv kept walking but threw another glance at the car. There was a beautiful dark-haired woman driving it. She'd heard stories about this woman too. Her friends were dead, and she was next.

Her thoughts were strangely rational considering she knew her life was moments from being over. There were two options. Get into the car knowing it would wreck at an extremely high speed or continue walking and allow the car to plow her down.

She stopped and inhaled deeply. The car braked next to her. Liv opened the door and sat in front next to the woman, clicking her seatbelt in place out of habit because it was going to prevent anything the lady of the woods had in mind. The car's speed didn't increase past the limit, and the driving never became erratic.

The dark-haired stranger drove her into Appleton and stopped at a gas station. Liv ran inside to use the restroom, but when she came back out, the car was gone. On the sidewalk near the freezer filled with ice for sale was her bag. She picked it up and walked across the street to the restaurant.

It would be almost impossible for her to eat, but she needed something in her system. She ordered soup and iced tea, taking her time, swallowing one small spoonful before psyching herself up to eat another. Her cell phone laid on the table with the screen facing up, and she stared at it. She knew as soon as she saw the lady, but she couldn't help but hope. One of them could've made it out alive.

An hour passed, and she still hadn't finished her bowl. The soup had cooled off, and a film covered the top of it. She had stirred it in several times, but it kept coming back, making it more unappetizing each time.

She went to the counter and paid, wondering what she should do. It could be years before any evidence was discovered if anything ever was. She'd go through a lot of scrutiny and be the butt of more jokes than she ever had been with those three. Still, it was the right thing to do. Before she left, she asked for directions to the Appleton Police Department. They'd believe her. Too many of the cases she'd heard about involved their PD for them to not believe her.

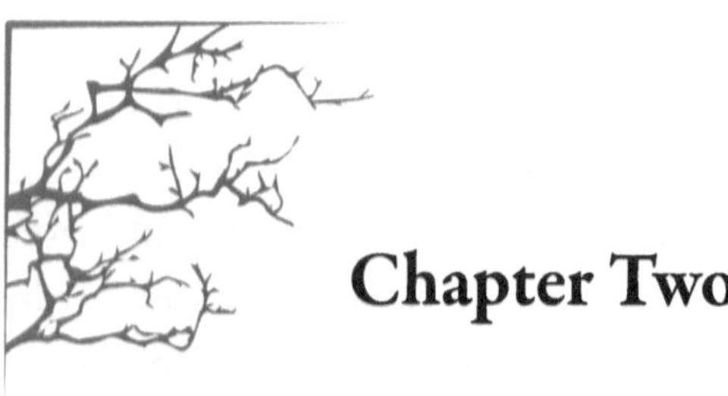

Chapter Two

Questions without Answers

The first memory Lorelei had of the Lady of the Woods she couldn't have been more than three years old. Everyone told her it was impossible for her to remember that far back, but she did. She saw the lady appear, watched her as the air changed into a beautiful woman with long black hair, and she smiled with excitement because she recognized her. That's the basis of her memory. Simply watching as the lady materialized in the clearing.

The reason she is certain she was younger than three is because she was clutching her old teddy to her chest when it happened. It was a teddy bear she had since birth and carried with her at all times, dropping it in the dirt, taking it in the bath with her, taking it to bed. It was worn, torn and tattered, and according to her parents, it reeked. No matter how much they washed it, Lorelei would have it smelling like rotting garbage in record time.

On her third birthday, her parents gifted her a new teddy bear, and she never saw her old one again. That's her second oldest memory. She was bawling with a party hat on her head while guests stood around awkwardly debating about coming up with excuses to leave early. "Dedee," she cried over and over as she searched for him.

Lorelei begged her parents for weeks to give him back. She threw the new teddy bear down every time they gave it to her. Eventually, they stopped trying, and the teddy bear was tossed in the pile of other toys in her room where it became forgotten until she found it one day years later while cleaning her room. She tossed it in the trash where it belonged.

When she was younger, there had only been a handful of mornings when she missed out on going to the clearing with her mom and Yanyo Rose. All of those were because she was on an overnight out of time with her parents while they conducted business or attended a funeral except for one. On that morning when she was five, she had slept in. Her mom didn't wake her to go. When she realized her mom had already been and back, she threw a tantrum so obnoxious and for so long Yanyo Rose stepped in and took her because her mom refused to make a second trip.

The lady hadn't appeared earlier when the two women walked down the ravine, but she did when Lorelei went. It made her feel special, like she was the lady's favorite. Yanyo stayed in the clearing with her as long as Lorelei wished she played and giggled with the mysterious lady.

As soon as she was old enough to make the trek herself, she stopped going with her mom in the mornings. She wasn't exactly allowed to go on her own, but she heard it said once it was easier to ask forgiveness than permission. Her mom believed the loss of interest in the clearing was a sign of growing up and encouraged her daughter to enjoy what little freedoms she had before she came of an age when venturing to the clearing each day was no longer a choice.

What her mom didn't realize was she was still going, but

she waited with thinning patience every day until her mom returned. When she ran off to play, her mom never knew where she was going. Lorelei saw it as a sign of growing up as well. It was a sign of independence. She didn't need her mom to hold her hand while she walked the ravine wall anymore. Besides, the lady shared more with her when she was alone. The lady did favorite her, preferred her because she didn't make the trek out of obligation. Lorelei goes to the clearing because she enjoys being there.

A long time ago she tried to tell her mom the lady liked her better. Lorelei was mad for reasons she couldn't remember now and wanted to hurt her mom's feelings too. She thought it would make her mom upset, jealous because the lady fancied her daughter's company. Her mom wasn't fazed by it. "Of course, she does. The lady loves children."

When she insisted it wasn't just because she was a child, her mother scolded her. For several days, her mom lectured her on and off about what the lady really was. "Pure evil. The number of people she's murdered is staggering, and you're running around talking like she's your best friend!"

Her mom issued warning after warning about the lady and the woods too. Stories of what had happened on the property just in Lorelei's lifetime could fill a library according to her mother. "It's easy now when you're young and innocent, but there will come a day when you do the lady's bidding. We'll see how much you adore her then."

That's where she was headed now. She picked up the walking stick at the base of the stairs and thanked the woods for their generosity. The ravine wall had stopped being intimidating years ago. She practically ran along the narrow trail until the ravine opened on her right. It was filled with majestic trees barely visible from the top.

She weaved her way through the trees until she reached the circular formation of them standing tall protecting the secrets held within the clearing. Her hand raised above her head until her fingertips grazed the sapphire pendant out of habit, muscle memory, more than active thought. The trees closed around her when she entered, and she smiled. The lady had been waiting on her.

Lorelei sat crossed legged on the ground, and the lady sat behind her, playing with her hair. She loved to run her fingers through Lorelei's wavy, auburn locks. They'd sit for hours just talking while the lady braided her hair or pulled it up on top of her head. Whatever style the lady gave her, she'd keep the rest of the day.

Sometimes her mom would raise an eyebrow when she saw the new do, wondering how Lorelei managed it. Her mom never asked probably because she was afraid of the answer.

"Why doesn't the sapling grow?" It was a question she had asked easily over a hundred times without ever receiving a satisfying answer.

"It's how the trees want it."

"It's what keeps us young, isn't it?" The words slipped out without thinking. Lorelei knew it was.

"Yes."

"Why a blackthorn tree?"

"Why not?"

Lorelei sighed and stared at the border trees in front of her. There had to be something special about it. "They're associated with witches, you know?"

The lady didn't say anything.

"I looked them up. There are a lot of stories about blackthorns and all of them relate to witches. They also don't grow in this area."

"This one does," the lady said, grabbing another section of hair from the side of Lorelei's head.

"It's alive, but it doesn't necessarily grow."

The lady laughed. The melodic tones made Lorelei smile.

She stopped herself from asking if the lady was a witch. It had already been voiced, and the lady seemed hurt by it. "Is that why Ravenwood is how it is? This sapling is connected to witches somehow."

"Anything can serve a witch," the lady said.

It was another non-answer. She figured out a while back she had to ask an exact specific question if she hoped to get the information she wanted. The hard part was figuring out exactly how to word it.

"Why a blackthorn tree? Why not an oak or a maple? Why was this tree chosen to be the centerpiece?"

There was no response, and Lorelei felt defeated. She had asked this question so many times, and in so many different ways. Either the lady didn't have the answer, or Lorelei was never going to figure out how to get the information.

"I don't know why."

It surprised her to hear the lady say that. There were very few times the lady admitted to not having all the knowledge the universe had to offer.

"Probably because I always loved them."

"Blackthorn trees?" Lorelei had never seen one except in books when she tried to find the secrets of the clearing on her own.

"Yes. They were always so beautiful with their white flowers and dark berries. I could never adorn themselves with the flowers, turn the berries to drink, or even use the wood although it was sturdy for some projects."

"Why not?"

"Because the blackthorn was associated with witchcraft. People would think me a witch!"

The two of them laughed together hard. The lady finished off the braid, wrapping the ends in elastic, and they laid on their backs staring at the ceiling of branches above them.

Lorelei flipped through the notes in her mind about everything she had tried to learn in the past. Ravenwood consumed her every waking thought. It would be so much easier if the lady would just start at the beginning and tell her everything, but it didn't work that way.

"Why the Weavers?" Lorelei asked changing tactics to find out something new.

"This is Weaver land. It has always been owned by them."

"Yes, but why build all of this out of it?"

"You mean the inn?"

"Yes."

"The trees were bored. Very few people ventured to this area. The people needed a reason to come."

"But why the Weavers?"

There was silence. Lorelei had just asked that question. The lady wouldn't answer it again.

"Why trap them here? Hold them hostage?"

"Is that what you think I'm doing?" The lady sounded hurt.

"Isn't it?"

"They are allowed to leave," the lady said assuredly.

"But you can reach them. You force them to come back."

"I can't force them to do anything." The lady sounded even more upset. "I remind them of where they belong."

"How far is your reach? I know you've been as far as North Carolina before."

"I can reach to the ends of this world." The lady chuckled and added, "And into worlds you don't know exist."

This was telling. It was extremely rare for the lady to include additional tidbits Lorelei hadn't directly brought up. She knew from experience if she took the bait and inquired further, the conversation would end.

"What is the power source of Ravenwood?"

The lady said nothing. Lorelei couldn't remember having asked this question before, but the lack of response told her she had. She had brought it up so many times, and in so many different ways, wanting to know who controlled what: the lady, the sapling, or the woods.

After a few minutes, the lady spoke. "I can't tell you about the source, but I can tell you this." The lady shared with Lorelei a rather wordy tale of events connected to this exact spot long before it looked as it does today. When she finished, the lady rose to her feet, signaling their time in the clearing was over.

"Why the Weavers?" she tried again. "Why not someone else? Why is no one allowed to sell it? They've had offers."

"The Weavers used to be a good family."

Lorelei's mouth flung open as she looked at the lady with widened eyes. Her family was good. They had tended Ravenwood for over a century.

The lady smiled softly and explained, "Long before I met

your Yanyo, the Weavers were a good family until they turned their back on their own because what others thought of them became more important than their blood. When they did it again, this time to your Yanyo," the lady looked off wistfully.

"You're talking about when you met her."

The lady nodded. Her eyes glistened with the tears she held back. "They sent her and their own son out here knowing they would perish. I fought for them. Being indefinite caretakers of this land was part of the deal we struck."

"Who struck?" Lorelei sat on her knees eagerly waiting to learn the identity the lady answered to.

"The deal I struck with your Yanyo and her husband Joseph to save not only their lives, but their unborn twins."

"Twins?" Lorelei asked in shock.

Lorelei trudged back to the inn making the walk stretch as long as she could manage. Each Weaver woman was only allowed one child, always a girl. She had chosen her future daughter's name and changed her mind to something else at least a dozen times. *'Yanyo had twins?'*

There was family out there somewhere. She had various distant cousins and other relatives on her dad's side. Yanyo's family who survived the war stayed in Europe and eventually she lost touch with them. The Weaver relation wanted little to do with the Ravenwood side of the family tree. Her parents sent the obligatory Christmas cards and attended funerals out of a sense of duty, but Lorelei was fairly sure no one wanted them there.

If Yanyo had twins, that meant someone escaped. Someone left Ravenwood and had a family of their own. She had people she didn't know existed. There was an entire branch of

Ravenwood she'd never met.

'Unless one of the babies didn't make it.'

Lorelei stopped at the bottom of the stairs and returned her walking stick to its place next to the one that had belonged to her Yanyo. She reached out and wrapped her fingers over the top of it, missing her Yanyo now more than ever.

When the lady mentioned twins, she just assumed one had been allowed to move on. It never occurred to her one passed away. If only her Yanyo was still here, she might be able to find out what happened. It wouldn't be an easy topic to bring up, but she'd figure out a way. Yanyo wouldn't have thought twice about the lady telling her.

The only person alive who might know about the other child was her mom. It would be next to impossible to say anything to her. If her mom found out she was going to the clearing on her own, she'd find a way to put an end to it.

It left her with the lady of the woods. She could add twins to the already overwhelming list of things she wanted to ask about.

The baby probably didn't make it. Healthcare was different now. It was much more common to lose a child in Yanyo's time. Twins had to increase the odds. Besides, someone would've slipped up about it. At some point, something would've been said in passing that should've been kept secret. It's how Lorelei picked up on most of the secrets her parents tried keeping from her.

If the child had lived, someone had to raise it. Lorelei heavily doubted any of the distant Weaver kin took the baby in to their home. No one ever tried to track them down to find where they came from, so no, the baby must not have lived.

She was about to the courtyard, and she looked around to see who was nearby. There was no one in view. The inn was almost completely booked, so it was strange there was no one outside. The courtyard drew plenty of attention.

Lorelei glanced at her watch and laughed. It was barely eleven. Some people were checking out about this time to head on their way. Others wouldn't start checking in for a few hours yet. Sometimes she forgot how slowly time moved in the clearing.

The kitchen was quiet when she came inside. The staff who worked the breakfast buffet were done for the day. Lorelei helped herself to something without fear of being caught. Her mom was sulking somewhere, and Grandma Edit wouldn't leave the office until precisely noon.

She went into the pantry where the food for the guests was kept and searched through plastic bins until she found the chocolate muffins. The family ate in the kitchen and had oatmeal or toast sausage links while the guests got their fill of muffins and danishes. Some even pocketed extras for the drive to wherever their next destination. Lorelei never got the good stuff unless she snuck it, and she couldn't do it very often without the kitchen staff discovering someone was helping themselves.

Lorelei left the kitchen after tossing the last bite into her mouth and headed to the front of the inn. She could hear voices and followed them to the reception area. The door to the office was open, and the desk clerk was standing in the doorway.

Grandma Edit was talking to someone, multiple people. Employees were discussing the dark energy of Ravenwood with her. Everybody called it something different. Some called it energy; some called it a curse. Lorelei called it a power source.

Everyone had a different opinion of how the energy arrived on the property. Frank who worked security believed it had to do with witchcraft. His theory was the witches who were run out of Salem came to this area.

Lorelei tapped the desk clerk on her shoulder, and she stepped aside, allowing her to squeeze past her into the office. None of the other adults noticed her.

One of the housekeepers thought it was Native American. The indigenous people had cursed the land when the white man came and ran them off.

Her Grandma Edit was arguing with them she knew the curse predated all of that. When the colonists first arrived to this area and were still on friendly terms with the people who were here before them, they were warned about this area. It was interesting to hear Grandma Edit discuss it. She was typically the first to insist there was nothing strange going on at Ravenwood. One thing she did enjoy arguing was history especially when she knew she had the details straight.

"Whatever controls these woods has been here since the days of Pangea," Lorelei chimed into the debate.

All three of them turned to look at her. Her grandma's eyes narrowed at her. She had joined a discussion she wasn't invited to, but the worse transgression was interrupting adult conversation.

"What makes you say that?" her grandma asked.

Lorelei shrugged it off. "I don't know. A guess." She left the office to head upstairs to her room.

'How do I know?' she thought. *'Because the lady told me.'*

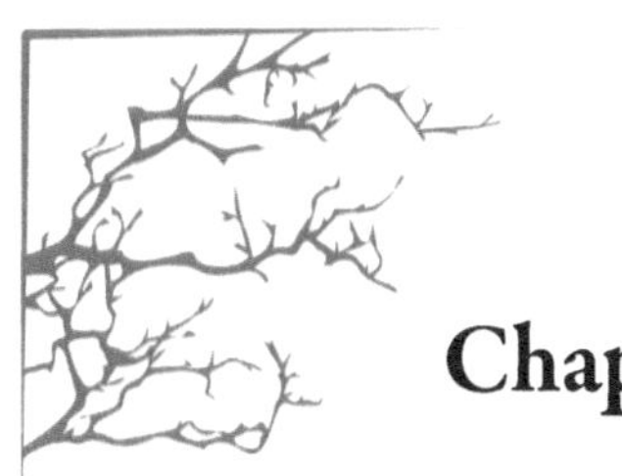

Chapter Three

All that Remains

Rosemary sat in the office remembering the last days before Edit left for college. She had opened the drapes to her bedroom. "Look at that view. The flowers in the courtyard are blooming. It's such a beautiful spring day. I love this time of year when life is renewed."

"Yeah," Edit grumbled from her bed. "Life."

She had been worried about her daughter for some time. Edit went through the motions without enjoying anything life had to offer. Even a life restricted such as theirs had plenty to appreciate.

Edit had rejected Ravenwood her whole life. They had shielded her from it as long as she could, wanting her to remain innocent and joyful until the truth crashed down upon her. Every daughter had been raised differently within these cold stone walls, and none of the Weavers had found a method which worked yet.

The rumors swirled around the property. There were always whispers of gossip from the employees and guests. It wasn't far into her teen years when Edit brought the subject up herself. "You don't believe in ghosts, do you?" She had scoffed at the idea there was anything more to Ravenwood than a few unfortunate accidents.

When Wilbur died, the official cause of death was a neurological event. Authorities believed something forced him to hallucinate which is why he tried to ingest the bark he ultimately choked on resulting in his untimely demise. His fragile state of mind also explained how he wound up under the bed. Everyone at the inn knew better. They knew the truth. The lady's reach didn't have limits.

This bothered Edit. She wanted answers about what happened to her father. No one was going to look into his death any farther because they believed it was the Ravenwood curse.

'It's not a curse; it's life.' Rosemary didn't share her thoughts with her only child.

Wilbur's death came at a time when Edit was realizing she couldn't have the life she dreamt about. The inn would be home for the rest of her life. She wouldn't be able to move away, travel extensively, or go to a college of her choosing. Her life was contained to the property.

When she sunk into depression, everyone assumed it was her father's death which made her despondent. Her mother had seen the seeds of depression sprouting within her daughter before Wilbur tried to run from the castle. His death wasn't the instigator, but it did push her over the edge.

Rosemary worried about her. She would later be accused of caring only about the inn. If Edit did something drastic, there wouldn't be a female descendant to take over the property. It cut her deeply to hear the rumors. She loved Edit deeply, and her well-being was all that mattered. They didn't know Edit wasn't the only heir.

If any Weaver woman found herself barren, there was a

backup plan. There hadn't been a Weaver yet who didn't pray for it, but it hadn't come to pass. Not having a child was the only way to remove yourself of the yoke the lady had on them, but it would not go well to trick her. Intentionally not getting pregnant wasn't an option.

"Come on, sleepy head," she sang out. "Time to greet the day."

Edit moaned and rolled on her side, pulling the blankets over her head.

'Maybe I shouldn't have forced her to go.' Rosemary questioned herself now, but at the time, she did what she thought was best.

"We leave tomorrow," she reminded her. "You need to pack and get ready."

"Why?" Edit groaned loudly.

Rosemary picked a few items of clothing off the floor, but there was enough for at least two loads of laundry. She let it all drop. "To have time to shop for everything you need before settling you in on campus."

Edit propped herself on her elbows. "No," she drew out the word. "Why do I have to go at all? Do I really need a degree to work here? Just teach me what I have to do."

Her daughter's beautiful long hair sat in a clump on top of her head. It had probably been a week since it saw a brush, longer since she showered. Rosemary couldn't get her to open up and discuss what was bothering her. It wasn't typical of the times back then, not like it is today. Instead of talking about what was bothering a person, other tactics were employed like steering them in a new direction or looking for little clues in things they said and did. It could be the death of her father alone weighing on her shoulders, or his death might've forced her to face the reality of the secrets Ravenwood held.

It wasn't far from the inn, and it wouldn't last forever. Still, college provided somewhat of an escape. She would meet new people, hopefully forge friendships, and maybe even find a beau. These years provided the most freedom she would ever have, and Rosemary drilled it into her daughter's head as much as she could.

The first semester showed no change. Edit barely passed her classes, didn't care for the professors or her classmates. She trudged along doing what she was expected to do barely existing in what she considered a doomed life.

Rosemary felt defeated. Her daughter was insisting on her mom picking a suitor. It wasn't the dark ages anymore. The sexual revolution had come and gone. Times had changed. Arranged marriages were a thing of the past, the wealthy elite past at that.

Everything was different when she met Edgar. He was certainly not from stock Rosemary would have chosen for her daughter, but he was the only one who could put a smile on her face. That had to count for something.

He didn't attend her college. He never attended any college. He was a service station attendant who was seven years her daughter's senior. There was nothing about this man Rosemary approved except Edit's happiness. For that reason, she kept her mouth closed whenever his name was mentioned. She hoped Edit would move on, that Edgar was merely a steppingstone to showing her she could still have a full life, but her hope quickly faded. The two of them were engaged before Edit graduated.

"Of course, he doesn't mind living here," Rosemary had scoffed alone in her room. "Even with the reputation, it's probably the nicest place he's ever rested his head."

Rosemary had to take the backseat to her daughter and the son in law she despised. Edgar was in it for something more than Edit's heart, but she couldn't prove it. If he was hoping there was money in the inn, he was sadly mistaken. Some years were better than others, but they mostly struggled to stay afloat.

It didn't take long for Edit to become pregnant. None of the Weaver women ever had difficulty conceiving. Edit was the first not to share in the joy of welcoming a new baby. The depression she had left behind when she met Edgar reared its ugly head and returned with a vengeance.

"Edit, this has to stop! Everything will be fine." Edgar's voice traveled down the hallway when Rosemary was heading to her room.

She stopped and turned toward their door. It was wrong to eavesdrop. As her husband, he was the one to guarantee Edit's well-being now, not her, but she couldn't help being curious.

"I'm tired of having this conversation," he said. "No, stop."

Whatever Edit was saying was too quiet for Rosemary to hear. She stepped softly down the hall, stopping at their door and rested her ear against the wood.

"I don't understand how this happened." Her daughter was crying. "We weren't trying to get pregnant."

Rosemary pursed her lips together and sighed. She returned to her bedroom and left them to their conversation. It wasn't polite to entertain such a private topic. Her daughter had learned about the birds and the bees. Intent is not always a necessary factor. If you mess with the bull, you're going to get the horns.

If she had stayed a few moments longer, she would've picked up on what was truly upsetting her daughter. They had other ideas. A plan they hoped to carry to fruition before having a family. It was the timeline which concerned Edit, not the child or becoming a mother.

The name Lucinda had been tossed around since Edit first learned the news. Edgar occasionally tried out a boy's name, but the women promptly ignored him. There was no guesswork involved here. The baby would be a girl. She would be doted on by the lady until she took over the reign at Ravenwood and would do the biding of the woods for the rest of her life.

The birth of her granddaughter had a positive effect on Edit. Even Edgar had never made her smile so freely. It only lasted a few years. Edit's spirits sunk once more and didn't return until Lucinda prepared for college herself.

Rosemary believed it was because Edit could step away from most of her duties. She hated everything the inn had to offer and was happy to pass the buck to someone else. If she had known what was really going on in her daughter's mind, she would've stopped them.

Edit led Edgar to the clearing one fall morning, claiming the lady invited him. Rosemary shrugged and went about her business. It wasn't common for the lady to allow the men folk into her arena, but it wasn't out of character for her to do so either. The two of them whispered and smiled as they passed through the courtyard resembling young lovebirds more than empty nesters.

Hours later, Edit returned alone. Rosemary watched from her window where she sat with her book. A sickly feeling knotted in her gut, but she remained calm. Her son in law never made his way out of the woods while she watched, and she continued to keep a look out for long after Edit had come inside. Something was terribly wrong. She knew it the moment she saw her daughter but held out hope she was merely overreacting.

She wandered down the hall, but their room was empty. It took close to an hour to find her. Edit was in the kitchen, sitting on the floor of the pantry.

Rosemary opened the door wider when she found her daughter, letting the light poor in the room over her. "Whatever are you doing, child?" she asked, shaking her head.

"I just needed a moment. That's all."

"Well, get off that cold floor before you catch a cold." Children never grow up no matter how old they get. "And where is Edgar?"

Edit didn't answer her mother, but she pulled herself up with the aid of the pantry shelves and shuffled out into the kitchen. She walked along the hallway as if in a trance playing with something in her hands.

"What is that?" Rosemary's irritation was about to boil over. "A leaf? You're playing with a leaf. What are you? Four?"

Edit looked at it sadly. "The lady gave it to me."

Rosemary stopped walking and watched as her daughter made her way up the stairs toward the family's wing. She pulled her shawl tight over her shoulders and went out the back door through the courtyard. At the edge of the trees, she stopped. Dusk draped over the sky, and she feared going into the woods in the dark by herself. She strained from side to side and stood on tip toe, but she couldn't see anyone.

"Edgar," she called quietly at first. There wasn't even a rustling of leaves in response. "Edgar!" she yelled as loudly as she could bring herself to do.

She turned to the inn and looked up at her daughter's darkened bedroom window. Not for the first time, she felt ill. Something kept Edgar from returning with his wife, and in these parts, it was a guaranteed bad sign.

Edit's sobs could be heard down the hall, and Rosemary nodded at the confirmation of what she knew all along. Edgar was gone. He was another in a very long line of souls lost to Ravenwood. She made the decision that night not to force Edit's hand. When she was ready, she'd share what happened. It would be decades later before Rosemary finally asked the burning question which had haunted her since Edgar disappeared.

Occasionally, Rosemary liked to visit the office. It had been years since she held an actual position at the inn. She did odd jobs here and there like overseeing the rearranging of the grand hall or helping to pick out designs for a remodel. It was busy work her daughter threw at her to keep her occupied, and she appreciated it.

Still, she missed her desk. It was Edit's now and had been for quite some time. The office looked exactly the way she left it except for one shadow box her daughter hung on the wall. Among other mementos, it contained her and Edgar's wedding bands, a suspended leaf, and a picture of their smiling faces on their wedding day adorned the back of the box. No one had to tell her it was the leaf Edit carried back with her from the woods that fateful morning.

Edit's official story was her husband had run off. If anyone asked, she'd tell him he was a lousy skirt chaser, and she was better off rid of him then she ever was with him. The sadness and emptiness in her eyes while she spoke told another story if anyone happened to pay her enough attention. Even so, they'd simply believe he had hurt her deeply.

The office was empty, so Rosemary sat at the desk. She remembered the days when she ran the show. Not too many women were allowed the positions her family had held. It was something which made her proud. It was probably the one good to come from being born a Weaver.

Her daughter's voice could be heard outside the door talking to the desk clerk. Rosemary barely jumped from the chair before her daughter entered the office. Edit was very protective of her privacy and didn't like anyone messing with her things. That included her mother and definitely meant her desk. Rosemary did the only thing she could to not appear suspicious; she studied the shadow box on the wall.

"Mother?" Edit said surprised. "I didn't know you were up."

Rosemary waved her off. "I couldn't sleep."

"So, you came to spy on what I was up to?" Edit huffed.

"I took a walk," Rosemary defended herself. "My feet found their way here on their own." She turned to look at her daughter, but as her eyes trailed across the items in the shadow box, she noticed something for the first time. It sent a shiver down her spine.

"Edit," she whispered, feeling all the air leave her lungs not to return. "This leaf."

Her daughter shoved past her and sat at the desk. "Don't you have something you could be doing? Needlework?"

Rosemary was frozen in place, staring at the veins on the leaf. Every leaf is different, just the same as snowflakes. Never had she seen one capable of spelling out a word, but at Ravenwood, the impossible happened every day. The leaf clearly read, "Edgar."

"Why does it have your husband's name?"

There was a small gasp from her daughter followed by a quiet sniffle. "I'm very busy, mother. We can discuss this later."

"No," Rosemary said, taking a seat across the desk. "We will discuss this now. What happened in the woods that day?"

Edit stared blankly at her mother.

"The day the lady invited Edgar to join you. Tell me," she insisted.

Her daughter's firm expression broke, and so did the dam holding back her tears. Rosemary consoled her as she sobbed heavily while the morning escaped them, grieving Edgar for perhaps the first time. When Edit did begin to speak, the story she wove filled Rosemary with regret for not taking a more authoritative role in her daughter's life.

"There's a way out, you know." It was the first thing Edgar told her after learning who she was and the property she was tied to. "Curses always have a reversal. You just have to find it."

This is why she chose him. It was the basis of their entire relationship. Edgar knew how to reverse the curse, or at least, he promised he could find out how to do it. Their plan was to marry while he acquired everything needed. They would wait to have children until after Ravenwood was free of evil then the place would be theirs. They could sell it and move far away from the ghosts of the Weaver past. Edit could finally travel to all the exotic places she had previously only read about in books.

"It took him longer than expected to find it," she said softly.

"Because it doesn't exist," Rosemary added.

Edit nodded absent mindedly like she had since figured that out on her own. "Then one day he announced he had it. He was so excited. All he needed was the branch of a tree, a specific tree."

"Blackthorn," Rosemary said.

Edit's eyes widened. "How do you know that?"

"Because," Rosemary released air out over her teeth making a whistling effect. "The sapling is a blackthorn tree."

Her daughter didn't move a muscle. She didn't know what the sapling was. That was evident. Rosemary only knew because Yanyo Rose mentioned it a time or two in passing. Edgar had definitely done some research before attempting this nonsense.

"What happened when you brought him to the clearing?" she asked. It was a miracle the trees standing guard even let him through their borders. They were expecting him, had to be. Nothing could be put over on the woods.

"He just..." Edit shook her head with a far off look in her eyes. The tears returned to her cheeks.

"Disappeared?"

She shook her head. "More like he evaporated." Edit's voice broke. "Pieces of him floated off on the breeze, and this leaf fell where he had stood."

"What did the lady do?"

Edit sat in silence.

"Tell me. This wouldn't have gone unpunished. Edgar was

not the only one behind this maddening attempt."

She shook her head. "It was a simple threat." She inhaled deeply and fidgeted with the blotter on her desk. "Not to step out of line again."

Rosemary didn't believe her.

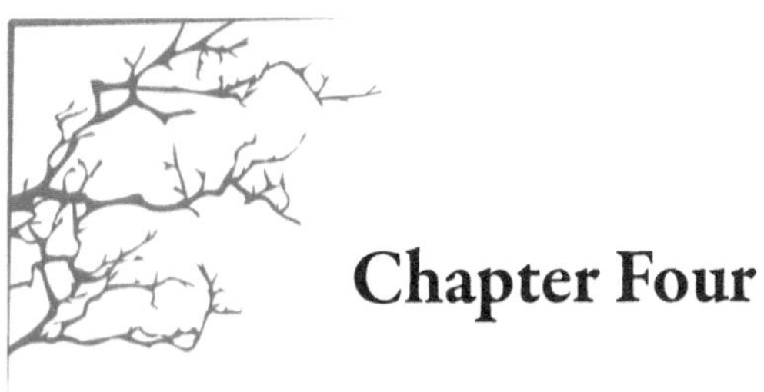

Chapter Four

Give the Dog a Bone

It was all the dog's fault. Buffy wasn't the reason they got lost in the middle of nowhere Massachusetts, but everything that happened after the car pulled over was because of her. Forty years later, the effects remain. Becky refuses to take a short cut, won't dare take the scenic route, and hasn't owned a dog since. A small fear of dogs took the place of the love she once held for the gentle companions she'd owned her entire life.

It wasn't poor Buffy's fault, but Becky couldn't help it. If there had been no dog that day, there'd be no memories waking her in the middle of the night in a cold sweat. She wouldn't spend her days daydreaming nightmarish scenarios of the fate she and Tom could've endured. Ravenwood wouldn't be a time suck draining her precious free moments in research on the property. It was almost like she believed if she could untangle the web of secrets shrouding the place she might find peace.

Tom and Becky had left her parent's house at the way too early hour of not enough coffee. Darkness shrouded them until the first hints of lighter blue appeared around Worcester. It would be their last trip home for the foreseeable future. School would be back in session, and so would Becky. One week later, Tom started his new job, and it would be a full year before he had any paid time off to go anywhere. They decided to take the backroads through the state, visiting a few places holding dear memories on their way to say one last goodbye to friends in Schenectady before heading to their new home in Pittsburgh.

Of course, none of their romantic, idyllic thoughts of reminiscing through the countryside took into account nothing was open this time of the morning. It was fine, really. Becky's nerves had been wound tight and were ready to break into a full blown panic attack at the drop of a hat. The direct route would've been better she realized quickly on the drive, but it was too late to say something to Tom about changing her mind. He'd insist the drive would relax her. If that was true, her uneasiness wouldn't have been increasing since they left.

They made a wrong turn somewhere around Cheshire and hadn't been on track for an hour. Since then, Tom had been steering the car down the backroads aimlessly. There was a map in the glove compartment neatly folded and ready to help, but the mere suggestion of it infuriated him. He didn't need the map because he wasn't lost. The fog didn't help either.

'He made a wrong turn.' Becky corrected in her thoughts. *'He's the world's greatest navigator if you listen to him tell it.'*

The tension was already building between them without either one saying a word regarding their current directionally challenged circumstances. She thought it was her anxiety rearing another one of its ugly heads at first, but it was Tom's frustration with himself causing the thick hanging air between them. It was made worse when the fog rolled in.

The light mist sweeping across the highway was quaint at first. It reminded Becky of cobwebs clinging to the corners of a room. Soon Mother Nature would brush it away as she did in her cleaning, and the landscape would be renewed with a dewy glow. The mist had barely settled over everything in view when it thickened into the densest fog they had ever seen.

Visibility was next to zero. Tom had a heck of a time keeping the car in his lane. He slowed to a near halt out of concern before pulling the car off the road altogether. They hadn't seen anybody for miles between the hour of morning and the country drive there was no one out.

He slammed his hand on the steering wheel before getting out of the car. Becky knew he'd return saying he was checking on this or that, or perhaps, decided to create his own facilities while opportunity presented itself. The truth was he was muttering and cussing his irritation under his breath to prevent Becky from hearing. He was avoiding an argument, and for that, she was thankful.

After enough time had gone by for him to clear his head, she figured if they were going to be stopped, it would be good for all of them to stretch their legs. She dug in the bag on the floorboard for the bowl she was using for Buffy. There was a milk jug she'd emptied at her parents and filled with water. She set the dish near the front tire on the shoulder, filling it halfway then opened the door for the dog.

Buffy wouldn't leave the car. It was like she was scared of the fog. Becky had to coax her off the seat and gently pull her onto the ground. Once she nuzzled up next to Becky, she seemed fine and lapped at her drink enthusiastically.

"Tom!" Becky yelled. She couldn't see more than a foot past the car.

"Yeah." She heard him reply from a distance.

Buffy's ears perked up, and she cocked her head to the side, studying something deep in the fog out of view. Becky reached down patting her head and scratching the back of her neck. Buffy's tail started wagging, and she stood up, circling around excitedly.

"What is it girl?" Becky asked. "Smell something?" There was probably a rabbit or squirrel nearby, and Buffy was hoping for the chance to make a new friend even if the poor, unsuspecting creature didn't consent.

"Sit," Becky told her. Buffy was inching her way into the fog. The dog came back to Becky's side, but didn't sit down.

"Sit, Buffy!" Becky said sternly.

The dog listened this time, but was back on her feet in seconds. "No, Buffy. Sit!" Buffy barked at her then took off into the fog.

"Buffy," Becky called, patting her leg. The dog didn't return.

Tom's voice made her jump out of her skin. "Damnedest thing I ever seen." Becky turned in the direction it came from, but she still couldn't see him. "About fifty yards down, the fog just disappears. It's bright and sunny. Looks like there's an invisible wall." He materialized through the cloudy vapor looking gray and drab until he stood next to his wife.

"Let's go," he said, walking around the front of the car to the driver's side.

"We have to get Buffy first," Becky told him. Her husband wasn't going to be happy about the dog running off, and it would make the rest of the drive even more unbearable.

"Buffy? She's not in the car?"

"No, I gave her some water, and she took off."

A stream of words best not repeated in public sprang from

his mouth. There would be an argument later over this. Becky couldn't see him, but she heard him hit the top of the car several times in frustration.

"What were you thinking, Becky? You can barely see your hand if you outstretch your arm."

"She's never done anything like this before. Why would I think she'd run off now?" Becky peered along the fog hoping to spy the dog somewhere close. "Besides, she's probably right around us. You know she doesn't venture far."

Tom walked about and joined her once more. They stayed a couple steps apart, keeping each other in sight. "There!" Tom cried.

Becky couldn't see anything save for half her husband's body.

"I see her tail. Buffy!" he called, walking forward.

He disappeared, and Becky panicked. She ran toward him until they collided.

"What are you doing?" he asked.

"I couldn't see you anymore. I got scared."

Tom rolled his eyes and clicked his teeth. "Just stay with me," he said. "You see her? She's right there," he pointed. Half his arm was swallowed by the fog.

Becky looked and could barely see the end of Buffy's tail wagging. It swirled the fog around like a cloud of smoke. Then she was gone again.

He took another step forward, and Becky followed close behind. She kept one hand on his back to prevent losing him. They continued on like this for a good ten minutes. They'd no sooner catch sight of Buffy, and then she'd vanish. Tom would follow after her with Becky at his heels. Trees would leap up out of nowhere in the fog, making Becky jump while Tom chuckled at her skittishness.

Their dog was acting strange. Her tail continued to wag. Sometimes she'd circle around showing visible signs of interest. There was an occasional playful bark. This wasn't an animal she was chasing. When Buffy was on the hunt, she moved slower, stealthier, and she didn't make a noise. It was like she was following someone else's command who was leading her on with a toy or a treat.

Becky was curious, but not enough to make her want to stick around and find out. She regretted following Tom into the woods and wished she was still at the car, waiting for him to return. She wanted to grab Buffy and make it back to the road never once stopping to think about if they'd even find their way in the fog.

Buffy finally stopped and sat down. The vaguest outline of her ear could be seen with one pulled back sharply, cutting through milky white vapor surrounding them. Whatever the dog was staring at was hidden by the fog, and Becky was thankful she couldn't see it.

"C'mere, girl!" Tom called and whistled.

Becky patted her leg trying to encourage her, but Buffy didn't turn her head.

Tom took a step forward and cried out in pain. A downed tree was blocking his path, and he kicked it with his foot when he took a step. He put his hand on it and felt along its side to the end, walking down its length to circle it.

They kept their eyes on Buffy and watched her continue to display odd behavior. She raised a paw, sat up on her haunches, laid down, and rolled over. She was shuffling through her full gamment of tricks as if someone was ordering her to showcase her abilities. Neither of them had seen another soul besides themselves and the dog.

"I take back what I said earlier," Tom whispered. His eyes didn't break away from the show Buffy was performing for a single moment. "That's the damnedest thing I've ever seen."

They finally made their way around the tree when Buffy disappeared once again. "Dammit!" Tom grumbled.

The next few steps were much slower. Tom waved his hands through the haze for obstacles before moving his feet having learned his lesson. They looked right and left, but they couldn't see her.

"Buffy!" Becky yelled. Tom expertly whistled for the dog, but there was no response.

Turning in circles, they'd occasionally stop and squint in one direction or another, hoping to catch sight of her or get an inkling about which way to go. The fog began to slowly dissipate. As it receded, their visibility improved, and they spied Buffy about ten yards away, laying down contently digging into something. Calling for her did nothing to break the dog's concentration. Buffy wasn't listening to any of their commands.

When they walked up to her, the last of the mist swirled no higher than their ankles. Both of them froze when the object of their dog's attention came into view. Buffy was gnawing on a leg. It was the lower leg bones still partially covered in flesh and wearing a shoe. As horrific a sight as it was, they soon realized there was more. Scattered in a small area around their dog was the rest of the body. It was partially decayed and partially scavenged. Even in its deteriorating state, they could see it was the body of a young man. His glasses crookedly resting of what was left of his face. Becky was no expert, but the body couldn't have been there more than a couple weeks.

Tom grabbed Buffy by the collar, and she growled. It wasn't like her. "Drop it, Buffy," he ordered at the dog. She wasn't letting go of her find.

They led her back to the car with the leg still in her mouth. Becky followed crying because her emotions didn't know what else to do. She was mortified, shocked, confused, disgusted by the sight she had just been subjected to, and it overflowed inside of her released in the form of tears.

By the time they returned to the car, the fog was gone. Tom coaxed Buffy into the car much easier than Becky had been able to get her out.

"You're not letting her keep that are you?" Becky asked terrified.

Tom straightened with his back to her. He was mad at her. This whole mess was her fault as far as he was concerned. "She's protective of it, and I'm not about to get bit. Especially not when there's a chance of rotting flesh being mixed into the bite."

He walked around the car, leaving Becky standing alone. She was making the careful consideration of whether to join them for the ride or walking to the nearest train station.

Before getting in the car, Tom told her, "I want you to prepare yourself. They say once a dog gets a taste of human flesh, they're never the same. We might be forced to put her down for this."

The thought made Becky sob harder. On top of everything else, she may lose her best friend, and it was her fault. She should've never let the dog out in the fog. Buffy never strayed in the broad daylight with a cloudless sky. It didn't add up for her to take off in bad conditions.

"We'll go to the nearest police station. They'll get the leg from her." Tom slipped into the car and the low roar of the engine quickly followed.

Becky didn't move. The road began to sway, and she lurched forward resting a hand on the top of the car afraid she might pass out. The air she breathed was thick like the fog which still enveloped her and hurt her lungs. She heard the revving of the engine and knew it was Tom signaling both his anger and eagerness to get this behind them.

They left the water dish on the shoulder to mark the location. Tom pulled the car back on the road. "Get the map out of the glove compartment," he told his wife. "The next road sign you see, I want you to figure out where we are and where the nearest town is."

Tom didn't use maps even though he always made sure to have one handy. When they traveled, he'd buy one for every state they passed through as soon as he crossed the state line. They'd pull over whether they needed a rest break or not just for the purchase. Not just that, he didn't appreciate a woman giving him directions. If she messed this up, she'd not only solidify his belief women were incapable of finding any place but the kitchen when it was time to fix supper, but she'd never hear the end of it.

Becky only spoke when absolutely necessary. She scoured the map like it was life or death, and this large, awkwardly folded piece of paper determined her fate. She saw the Route 116 sign and found it on the map easily enough, but her internal directional system was faulty at best. Tom had made a left hand turn not long before they stopped. She was almost certain. That meant they were headed west. "There's a town straight ahead," she told him. She exhaled the breath she didn't realize she'd been holding and hoped she was right.

"How far?" he asked, glancing at the gauges on the dash. Luckily, the sign declaring Appleton was six miles away appeared in time to save her from having to figure it out.

A short while later they arrived in Appleton. Becky waited in the car until the racket made by Buffy's chewing became too much to bear. Her ears were hypersensitive to the sounds. Each time Buffy's jaw closed on the leg, or a bit of drool dripped in a string from her lips until it broke free and fell on the seat or floorboard, the noises made were amplified and echoed in Becky's head. She stepped outside the car and waited not aware how much she needed the fresh air until she took a deep breath.

Tom went inside the police station. He explained to the desk officer what happened in the country, and their dog refused to let go of a piece of the victim. An officer accompanied him to the car. Becky could hear their conversation as they approached. Tom was worried about how they'd be able to get the dog to give up the leg. The officer opened the rear door, and Buffy tossed the leg on the ground at the officer's feet and sat upright, wagging her tail.

They were able to keep Buffy. The question of her fate was never brought up. For a long time after that day, Becky saw the young man's face every time Buffy's tail began to wag.

Sometime later they received a letter from the Appleton Police Department thanking them for their help in solving a missing person's case. They identified the young man simply as "Aaron."

That tidbit stayed in the back of Becky's mind for the rest of her life. The letter followed her around in a box in storage and occasionally she'd come across it, not that she needed anything to remind her of that day. Then one day a fancy new invention came into everyone's home. With the help of the World Wide Web, she hoped to discover more information.

Becky learned all about Ravenwood. She and Tom had been lucky to survive. Every internet search she did for as long as she lived gave her the same result. There was only ever one Aaron she came across whose body was discovered on the property. One of the searches included a photograph. It had been decades since that day in the western Massachusetts countryside, but some things can't be forgotten. The image of his haphazard glasses resting on his decaying face was never far from Becky's thoughts. She recognized him immediately. He had gone missing at the age of nineteen in 1956, twenty-one years before she and Tom had stumbled upon his remains.

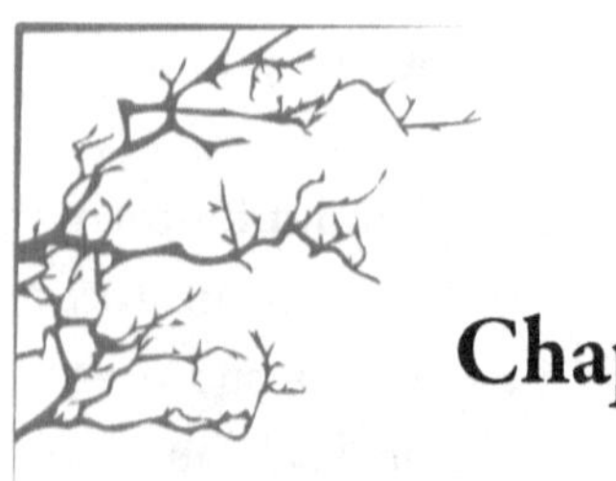

Chapter Five

Testing Theories

Simone had a theory. Since no one was going to listen to her, she was going to have to prove it herself. The claims that a piece of property was somehow cursed, and the woods would take a life for transgressions such as pulling a leaf off a branch were ridiculous at best. Curses, witchcraft, voodoo, all of it was just a bunch of hocus pocus. By that, she meant it belonged in the movies.

There was no proof any of it was real. The most a curse could do was become a parasite in the mind causing the host to create the outcome out of fear. Ravenwood wasn't cursed, but there was something sinister lurking in the woods.

Researching the land was tedious. It was hard funneling out fact from the fiction. Even the most well written articles were filled with nuiances of myth and legend. There were a dozen accredited sources with a dozen different totals of how many had gone missing or lost their lives in these woods. Part of that was due to shoddy police work. Too many deaths had been chalked up to bear attacks or unusual accidents. Part of it was because Ravenwood had grown into its own monster over the years.

Someone might go missing during a morning jog in Northern California. After a couple years, it would be chalked up to Ravenwood. Either someone would speculate the person had left the area to take a break winding up on the other side of the country, or they would claim Ravenwood's reach knew no bounds.

Simone parked her car at the Shaw Memorial Park. She secured her meticulously packed hiking backpack over her shoulders and around her waist before setting off on the trail. It was her first time visiting the park or anywhere close to the woods at the center of all the attention. Someone she had met during her research had tipped her off to this back access way.

There's supposed to be a well-worn route through the trees between the three quarter and one mile markers. Her source was going to come out yesterday and mark the spot for her by tying a ribbon around a tree, so she wouldn't miss it. She hoped they followed through, but if they didn't, she'd figure it out. With her GPS and hiking aps programmed for the property already, she'd find it on her own.

For the last two weeks she had tried to find someone to come out and explore the woods with her. It wasn't because she was scared like her friends who teased her relentlessly accused. Good company would be appreciated. The long hours would pass quicker with someone to talk to while she explored. None of them had been willing to even come close to property's borders. They didn't believe in curses outright, but they believed in Ravenwood.

'How about that?' she thought. *'The local came through for me.'* The red ribbon tied to the birch tree fluttered in the breeze.

She opened the trail app on her phone and stepped into the woods. It had taken her a month to plot the layout of Ravenwood in her spare time. She had divided it into three sections, making grids to do a careful search over every inch. She would spend all day and the next two Saturdays exploring.

This wasn't her first time in the outdoors, and she was prepared for anything. Her trail pack contained everything she might need from a blanket, first aid kit, enough food to last for a week and emergency flares. There was also a knife latched to her ankle and a thirty-eight strapped to her side.

Her dad had taught her to be prepared for anything, and she was. To that end, she'd make sure she didn't ruffle the leaves on any trees while she was out here either. There was nothing to the legends, but it didn't mean she needed to test two theories at once.

The ravine was planned for in her grids. According to the maps, there was only one, but it was sizeable. The locals claim there were several smaller ones. Depending on if they were right and whether or not there were any other obstacles to climb over or around, it should only take one day to explore each section. If she didn't find what she was after by then, she'd come back out to walk the ravine.

It wouldn't be hard to find. Something like that could be noticed without having to dig around for it. If she never found it, she still wouldn't be necessarily wrong. She'd have to move on to Plan B.

There were too many disappearances out this way, and that was after filtering through the ridiculous claims where the victim had probably never stepped foot on this particular piece of land, let alone had ever been in the state. There was one thing most of the victims had in common. Something was always missing.

If the body was ever recovered, there'd be an object not

with them anymore. Sometimes it was a piece of jewelry, a wallet, or something valuable. Sometimes it was a shoe or jacket. The police chalked it up mostly to animals scavenging the remains and dragging items which got lost in the woods. It might be decay if the body took decades to be discovered. There was also the possibility the victim might not have actually been in possession of whatever the trinket was at the time of their death.

'Yet, it was always a bear or accident according to the police, and it was the cursed trees according to the area residents.' There was one creature of habit who liked to collect mementos: serial killers. The real threat in these parts was a murderer on the loose.

Not all of the victims were murdered by him. Some probably did succumb in a manner like the police suggested. The earlier disappearances were excluded from her theory as well. Either that or these woods had seen more than one Gacy over the years.

Simone believed there was a shack out here somewhere. The killer did his work on the scene because there was safety in an area where everyone was too afraid to go. If she found it, chances were the tokens he took to remember his victims were there too. There'd be enough evidence to convince the police without those because she doubted the killer carried everything away with him when he was done after scrubbing down his kill cabin.

This was his safe house. He'd leave everything he needed, and there was bound to be DNA evidence all over the place. Simone spent years diving into this research and always fantasized herself the hero who was instrumental to his capture. It had played out in her mind so many times, in so many ways. Sometimes a victim would be there, ready to meet her fate, but Simone would intervene. In other scenarios, the killer would return with his next victim after she brought the police to the scene.

All she had to do was find it. Take a few pictures of what was contained inside the murderer's lair. She might even bring something with her to the police station to back her claims. She'd be a hero. Her face would be plastered on the local stations that night, and across the nation by the end of the week as the body count began to rise. She was going to do what no one else had been able to, and it was right there, staring blatantly in their faces.

She'd been working this grid for several hours and stopped to take a break. The tree she sat under was full and robust. It cast shade enough for a small group to rest. Directly across from her stood a tree in its final days. It had long since lost its life force. The branches were bare with a few of them already missing, and the bark was a dull gray. It probably wouldn't make it the next winter before being uprooted by the elements.

On the trunk, she saw a face. It was a cartoon like image of a man wincing. Rings above his head gave the impression he was blowing his top. The more she looked at it, or rather the longer it stared at her, the more uncomfortable she became. *'Easy to see how the tales of these woods got started. A lesser experienced person would go mad out here.'*

Everything was packed away in her bag after she ate. There were some who would insist it was out of fear of the trees, but waste shouldn't be left in nature. She had always been a responsible hiker.

When she stood up, the face on the dead tree seemed to have moved. It wasn't straight across from her anymore, but had turned slightly. Simone shook her head. *I must have moved around a bit to the side when I put everything away.*

She continued her hike easily. There hadn't been too many obstacles in her way so far. This side of the property was considered the easiest to trespass. It was a contradictory claim. If so few survived the cursed woods, there shouldn't be enough information to make this statement.

The snapping of a twig behind her sent her feet flying in the air. She turned with her hand to her chest, expecting to find nothing more than a wayward squirrel. There was nothing, not as far as animals go, and certainly not another human. Instead, she looked behind herself to find a very unusual tree.

It was a dead tree with a cartoonish character's face on the trunk. If she didn't know better, she'd think the tree was following her. *'What am I thinking? It's not the same tree. I left that one over two hours ago. Even if I got turned around, the rest of the landscape has changed. It's more field now. The tree I sat under is nowhere to be seen.'*

This just happened to be a similar tree on all accounts. Two trees. Both dead. Both shaped alike. Both with matching cartoon faces in the trunk. She wasn't sure of the odds especially when it came to pareidolia, and she wasn't going to risk her mental state by looking it up.

'They were carved.' It came to her out of the blue. That explained why the faces looked identical. The bigger mystery was how she couldn't remember passing by the second dead tree.

Simone did her best to push it from her mind. There were

easily two to three hours of hiking for the day left, and her midsection was grumbling, yelling at her it required fuel if she wanted to proceed. The tree had shaken her up more than she cared to admit, and she didn't want to stop again. It wouldn't be too difficult to push through and eat when she returned to the car.

She continued on, following the directions she had programmed into her phone. There was an unnerving sense distracting her. She couldn't shake the feeling she was being watched. Every nerve in her body was on edge with heightened response. Part of her wanted to glance back, to see if anything, or anyone, was there. She refused to give in to it. This was exactly the kind of paranoia which caused people to get turned around and lost.

The sensation consumed her completely. A cold sweat broke out on her face and neck. Her breathing became labored. It would be easy to spot a shack in the woods, but her careful inspection of the landscape was lost to the unwavering belief she was being followed. She gave in to it at long last if for no other reason than to rid herself of it. Once she saw there was nobody there, she'd be fine to go on. Simone inhaled deeply and turned around. One hand rested on the grip of the gun at her side. No one was behind her, but there was a tree. It was a dead, cold, gray tree with a cartoonish man exploding from anger engraved on the trunk.

Simone stood frozen in terror. There were easily three dead trees at Ravenwood, probably dozens if not more of them. If someone was showcasing their artwork by carving it on trunks, then yes, there could be three trees with a similar etching. It was even a strong likelihood for her to happen upon those same three trees during one day-long hike. That's not what unsettled her.

'There's no way I passed by two of these dead trees without noticing them.' Time stretched out going painfully slow. She could hear the seconds of a clock tick off in her mind, but her watch was digital. *'That's what I did though, obviously.'*

She checked her phone. There wasn't much left for her to investigate today. She put her pack on the ground and dug around inside it until her hand felt her binoculars case. The plan had been to be thorough, to leave no stone unturned so to speak. Not anymore. She could finish off the rest of the area with the help of binoculars and head back to the hiking trails near where she parked her car now. *'A cabin is hard to miss,'* she reminded herself.

After they were hung from her neck and her bag positioned over her shoulders and fastened around her neck, she glanced one last time at the tree. It was gone. Simone let out a small whimper. She turned around and found it. The tree had moved again. It was no more than three feet behind her.

'No, I must've moved.' She took deep, concentrated breaths. After checking the tree was still where she left it, she began walking again, stopping every handful of steps to peer through the binoculars at the part of the property she wouldn't be hiking like she had intended.

Not once did she think the trees were coming to life, following her. It didn't affect her beliefs on whether this place was cursed. There was a logical explanation for what was happening.

As she walked, she considered the possibilities. The most likely was some abandoned mine or well giving off toxic fumes which could affect brain activity. That would also explain a lot of the disappearances and stories people told about what the trees were capable of doing. It was something to look into once she was out of here, breathing cleaner air, and thinking straight.

The next time she came out she'd bring some sort of tests with her to see if there was anything dangerous in the air. If she couldn't find anything which would provide instant results, she'd take the samples and send them off for analysis herself. She'd wait to cover the remaining sections until she knew it was safe.

If she had taken the time to consider the possibility what people said about Ravenwood might be true, she'd have thought about her actions since arriving that morning. She'd been careful. There was no unnecessary damage done to anything. Nothing was pulled off any branches. No flowers had been picked or trampled for that matter. She cleaned up after herself. There was no litter left behind.

As good as she was to nature, there were a couple areas where the terrain wasn't so easy. She beat a path through, not yet pushed to the point of wavering from her carefully plotted grid. Vines were cut. Underbrush was beaten back. It was definitely possible a couple branches were bent or even snapped as she cleared a path.

Simone stopped and grabbed the binoculars again. Without checking her phone, she guessed there was only about thirty minutes left on her hike, give or take. The closer she got to the end the more frazzled she felt. It was like she could sense the timer counting down, and she was almost out of time.

I've read too many stories about the legend, she mused, lifting the binoculars to her face. The view was blocked and blurry. She lowered them to check the lens, but it wasn't necessary. What she saw frightened her more than she'd ever experienced.

She screamed and fell back onto the ground. Her hand went back to catch her fall, and she heard the snap in her wrist when she landed. The pain in her arm was overshadowed by the shock she felt of seeing the same dead tree directly in the path of where she had been walking.

There was definitely something in the air. She checked her phone to make sure she was where she thought she was. *'Thirty minutes if I walk. Less than ten if I sprint.'* Surveying the property was done for the day. She needed to get back to her car.

Using her good hand for support, she pushed herself off the ground and knelt while searching her bag. There was a bandage wrap in the bottom of her bag. She was always prepared. Once her wrist was supported, she'd race back to the hiking trails.

Something was wrong. She couldn't put her finger on it while she dug through her backpack, but once she had the bandage wrap in hand, she noticed it. The tree was gone.

Simone lifted her head slowly, but she refused to take her eyes off her bag. Finally, she shifted her gaze. It really had disappeared. *'This place is toxic,'* she cringed. She wrapped her hand in a hurry, providing minimal support to the fracture. It was good enough. She'd fix it later.

The feeling of being watched returned. Her heart raced when she turned to see the same dead tree with the same cartoonish face behind her. She screamed, dropped her bag and ran. The tree appeared in front of her, and she turned to the right. It was there too.

She stopped and spun around in a circle. The tree was everywhere. Any direction she cast her eyes; she saw it. Her mind worked overtime trying to convince her it was a trick. She had been poisoned by whatever fumes were saturating the air.

There was a tap on her shoulder, and she held her breath. It was behind her now. One of the dead gray branches had touched her. She didn't notice the pain until she saw it. Movement from the corner of her eye caused her to look down. It hadn't simply tapped her; the end of the branch protruded through her flesh on the left side of her chest. One final blood curdling scream escaped her lips followed by silence.

Months later her backpack was found by someone who noticed something red off to the side of the trail at Shaw Memorial Park. It was the only evidence ever discovered after her car was found. The binocular case was in the backpack, but the binoculars were never recovered.

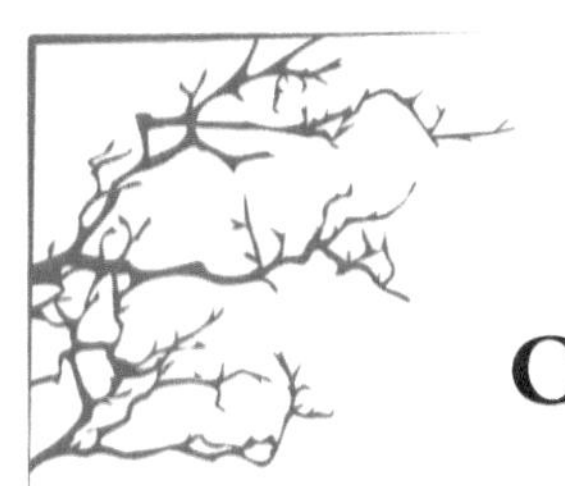

Chapter Six

Tree Sense

The rain outside danced on the windows creating its own music as it rat-a-tat-tatted its way onto the panes. The endless gray skies from the spring showers deepened Alice's mood. It had been a long day manning the desk. Today was the epitome of if it can go wrong, it will go wrong. Added to it was this all-encompassing dread she couldn't shake. She was positive there would be a body today, but she couldn't explain what caused her to feel that way.

The Talberts were spending a long weekend at the inn as they were prone to do when they were in the area visiting family. There was an era in the early days of Ravenwood when this castle was the height of elegance and charm. People came from all over the east coast to stay at this quintessential inn. The parties held in the grand hall were notorious and extravagant. Those days were short lived primarily due to the unexplained activity and disappearances. It had ended before Alice came to Ravenwood, but the stories and photographs from that era provided a different form of haunting.

Some people were rooted in the past however. The Talbert couple both had parents who regularly stayed here during that era bringing their kids along in tow. They considered themselves to be the personification of high class for their ability to afford the inn when more affordable accommodations were just down the road. This way of thinking had been instilled in them from a very young age. As parents now with children of their own, they parroted it.

The inn couldn't possibly live up to its previous standards, but here they were. They made the trip often to visit family or just take a long weekend to enjoy the rural part of the state and relax. They weren't the only family to stay here out of tradition. Some years, these second and even third generation patrons were what kept Ravenwood in business. If they had an opinion about the lore attached to the property, they kept it to themselves.

The only thing high class about Ravenwood today was the price tag. The inn had fallen into disrepair and was in much need of a makeover. It was far more than a fresh coat of paint or replacing the bedside lamps could cover. There were serious overhauls required to return the inn to its former splendor.

The patronage had declined. According to Mrs. Weaver, the money wasn't there. Alice worked the desk and knew how much money was coming into the inn. The math wasn't adding up on her end. Whenever she voiced these opinions to anyone, she was met with the same resistance. "You don't know what all goes into running a business like that. There's a lot more expense than you realize."

Alice was confident she'd covered all the bases, but she did have to guess the amounts. The insurance alone had to come with a substantial hit to the checkbook. Each incident added to the cost of coverage. Every time something happened, like say a young boy disappeared on the property, insurance likely had to pay a hefty sum.

The Talberts had just found their son who went missing before the rain rolled over the woods. For two hours, every available person was on a manhunt calling his name. From the front desk to the kitchen, all the occupied rooms were checked, empty rooms were opened and searched, to the walking trails on either side of the courtyard. It was like he disappeared into thin air.

"Roy!"

"Where are you?"

"The fun's over!"

"Time to stop playing!"

It excluded Alice. She was needed at the desk. The police had been notified, and while they would normally have a lackluster response of advising them to check every nook and cranny where a child might fit and wait until they opened an investigation, they came out to Ravenwood with a shocking response time. Out here one must never assume an expected outcome to a typical situation.

After two hours, the boy walked off the trail as though nothing was amiss. He regaled his parents with stories about how he had got lost. Never mind the minor detail of how the child could've become lost on a trail in the first place. Obviously the boy had completely disobeyed the rules and wandered off into the woods. He was lucky he saw his parents again. His youth was what saved him. The woods seemed to have a soft spot for the innocent.

Roy carried on about the kind woman who showed him the way back. His stories about her painted her as a saint, a guardian angel sent straight from the heavens to be his protector. He described her as having long black hair, but he couldn't remember what she was wearing. The police chalked it up to his age when talking to the Talberts, but their shifty glances to each other told the staff they were very much aware of who came to the boy's rescue.

The murmurings throughout the staff grew to a discernable level. While Mrs. Talbert searched for the mystery woman who saved her son, no one on the staff had the nerve to tell her it was the dark haired lady who came to his rescue. Finally Mrs. Weaver created a fake profile of a guest who checked out shortly after the boy was found safe. She didn't want any fanfare or accolades. Mrs. Talbert was disappointed not to have the opportunity to show her gratitude in person, but she was satisfied with the work of fiction fed to her by Mrs. Weaver.

The Talbert family, having missed their luncheon, loaded up and went to town to salvage the rest of their day. They might very well go the rest of their lives without realizing the true dangers their son could've faced.

That didn't calm Alice's nerves. It wasn't what the dread had been warning. There was something far more sinister on the horizon.

Prior to that, Alice slightly eavesdropped on Mrs. Weaver berating her daughter at the far end of the grand hall. She couldn't hear anything being said and knew Mrs. Weaver was unhappy anyway because it was her usual everyday mood. Additionally, her gestures provided other clues. The way her arms crossed tightly over her chest, the shaking of her head, the wagging of her finger let Alice know Lucinda was being reprimanded for something.

While Alice worked, she cast quick sly glances in their direction feeling sorry for the poor girl. Lucinda seemed to be in a state of constant discipline by her mother. Lucinda had enough on her plate without her mother trying to help which only served to make matters worse.

It was then Alice had the epiphany. Mrs. Weaver wasn't a person; it was a title. Each of the women before Edit and every Weaver woman after her would have to hold the title and carry out the same duties. They were born into a life of servitude to the woods, keeping the inn in business, bringing in new victims for the trees. The victims weren't always murdered.

'Am I not a victim myself?' Alice thought. *'One of many the trees have fed off since long before the castle was erected at Ravenwood.'*

The trees feed on your essence, your soul. They smother the spark a person has for life until the embers of that fire are barely warm. All of the joy once held are vanished.

Lucinda didn't want this life, and Alice couldn't imagine any of the Weaver women would have chosen this life if leaving were an option. A dark cloud followed the girl wherever she roamed, but Alice had never put much thought into it until today. The insight struck her midway through the lecture from mother to daughter. Lucinda might not make it.

'Then what?' Alice wondered. *'What would happen to Ravenwood if there was no longer a Weaver woman to endure?'* It was a revelation which held many possibilities. Some less ominous than others, but nevertheless, a revelation she didn't want to pursue for she was afraid of where her thoughts might lead. Watching the interaction, having the enlightened awareness didn't quell her dread, but it didn't add to it as well.

Before that, a poor mother from Boston stopped by the inn to drop off an eight by eleven, black and white, missing poster of her son. He looked older than twenty as his mother claimed. The date of birth under his picture on the paper in her hands proved he was barely an adult.

The woman explained to Alice the family had a reunion about thirty minutes south of Ravenwood. They left the day before their son Elton was able to go. He had finals to finish up at school, and he had decided he would drive himself after his last test. He never made it to the gathering, the motel, or any nearby family member's home. No one had seen him since.

Alice assured the woman she would make copies and hang the notice in the breakroom, at the desk, and anywhere people might see it. They'd give her a call immediately if anyone had any information which might help. The lies fell from her lips easily after years of practice.

'Look around!' she wanted to scream. *'There are no missing posters anywhere!'* The inn should be plastered with them. Odds are there would be enough to wallpaper the entire grand hall with faces of those lost, many of whom probably met their end somewhere on the grounds. She bit her lip and choked down all the words trying to escape.

She held the picture in her hand for a long time after the woman left, studying the boy's face and committing it to memory. She didn't recognize him, but most of the bodies removed from the property had never stepped foot inside the inn. They were lost travelers who made more mistakes than a simple wrong turn, trespassers who didn't understand the force contained in the woods, or adventurers wanting to test the powers of the trees.

Her heart went out to the mother who must be overwhelmed with guilt for not waiting until her son was ready before leaving. That one simple decision, if she had the power to go back and change it, would've prevented whatever fate was bestowed upon her son. It was something the woman would have to live with for the rest of her life.

When she heard the click clack of heels approaching from the kitchen, she crumbled the missing notice and tossed it in the trash bin under the counter. It's where Mrs. Weaver would order her to file it. Between the general public's assumptions every missing person within a five hundred mile radius had to be associated with these woods, and her belief a notice such as this one was bad for business, seeing it would anger Mrs. Weaver because Alice didn't toss it at once. Then she'd have to deal with her boss's wrath for the rest of her shift which had barely begun.

Still, the knowledge a body had been added to Ravenwood's running totals wasn't enough to dissipate her dread. No, she was certain there would be a physical body today. *I wonder what the story used to quell the fear and agitation in the guests will be this time.'* The inn had run out of fresh ideas and recycled old ones every time police cars and the coroner's van where called nearby.

It wasn't the first time she came to work with a feeling similar to this. The property alone was enough to cause gray skies to overcast her mind. This was different. She couldn't pinpoint it, and she'd never had a moment of psychic ability in her life. There was no other explanation for why she felt this way except to say she just did. It was like the woods had decided to give her notice, so she could prepare for the day ahead.

As soon as she arrived at work that morning, maintenance was at the desk in need of a room key. There was a flood in room eighteen. The water was dripping into the room below it. The extra work involved to get everything patched up and ready for the following weekend's full house meant it was already a bad week, and it was only Monday morning.

Luckily, the guests in the room below had awoke early and noticed the drip right away. If it had gone on much longer, the damage would have multiplied. The cause of the leak was an overflowing bathtub overhead. Maintenance didn't know for sure until he was able to get into the room, but his guess was correct.

He would use this incident to appeal to Mrs. Weaver for a skeleton key and would be immediately denied. There was no one at the front desk overnight except for certain times of the year. If someone came off the road late, the phone was on the counter with instructions of how to place the call. It rang to the security guard's office, and he'd be along as soon as possible. Because of this, he waited far too long – twenty minutes – until Alice arrived to receive the spare room key.

For the rest of the week, he'd mutter under his breath about the ridiculous circumstances he was expected to work around. Gone, at least temporarily, were the thoughts of the woods and putting his life in the hands of the trees whenever he punched the time clock. It was absurd to not have the key because his boss didn't trust men and wouldn't put it past him to stick his nose into rooms when he had no real business being there.

None of that would be complained to Mrs. Weaver. He'd appeal based on how it hindered his job having to wait. He took the key from Alice and headed upstairs already practicing what he'd say to her in his mind.

The guest was gone along with all her belongings. In

hindsight, the name Barb Smith might have been a made up moniker. Typically, fake names were used by illicit couples or someone up to no good. Her room key was left atop the small dresser along the wall, but nothing else remained in the room. People had tried to vandalize the property in the past, and they would do it again. It wasn't even the first time an overflowing tub had been left as a departure gift.

Alice had expected a body to be found in the tub. The reddened water diluted to a transparent pink. It surprised her to learn the guest had fled. She had been certain as soon as the maintenance man began speaking room eighteen was the cause of her trepidation.

The room was fit to let out once the water was sopped up. There was damage which required immediate attention, but it wasn't visible. Two rooms out of service at the same time would set Edit on the war path. Maintenance would repair the damage from the leak in the room below it then inspect the water damage done in the bathroom, repairing and replacing what was necessary.

When housekeeping cleaned the room, they did a thorough search as was customary in these situations. Even before what happened to Mrs. Weaver's father Wilbur, any room emptied without the guest stopping by the desk was given a complete search. Nothing was discovered.

Alice was stunned. She anticipated a body would be found under the bed or in the small closet. By the end of her shift, she accepted she had been wrong about what she thought would happen.

She checked in the last guests of her shift as her relief showed and prepared to take over. They were a young couple who were blissfully unaware of the trials and tribulations of life, let alone the sufferings of Ravenwood. "Enjoy your stay," she told the guests warmly. They walked up the wide stone staircase smiling in awe at the castle and each other.

There was a brief rundown of important notes to go over with her co-worker. Then she grabbed her things and pushed open the door marked private behind the counter to leave. Before the door closed behind her, she heard the scream.

It was an ear shattering, soul shaking shriek which caused her blood to run cold. *'There it is,'* she thought sadly. She was all too aware of what room they had been assigned. *'They found Barbara.'*

The dread which had consumed her all day faded and was gone by the time she reached her car. The clouds had moved past taking the rain with them. It was wet outside with a few puddles scattered around the lot, and there was a slight chill in the air. The sun had come out, making a brief appearance before it retired for the night bringing a cover of darkness to the woods once more.

Alice took a deep breath happy to be leaving before the show started. She opened her door and quickly pulled out of her parking spot. If Mrs. Weaver saw she was still on the property, she's have her stay to help navigate the police and more importantly, the reporters. They always found out whenever something dark occurred at the inn.

She drove down the lane and glanced in the rearview mirror which was not something she usually did, not here. The things she saw directly in front of her were horrid enough without finding out what may be watching from behind. This time she checked hoping she wouldn't find Mrs. Weaver running out of the inn after her.

It wasn't Mrs. Weaver who caught her eye. In the mirror, she could see the window of room eighteen. There was a young woman standing in it, watching her as she drove away. It wasn't the young blonde who had recently arrived, and it wasn't Barb Smith or whatever her real name might be either. It was a woman with flowing, long dark hair wearing a simple dark gray dress reminiscent of a different time. Alice wasn't sure if she was seeing things, but it almost looked like the woman was waving.

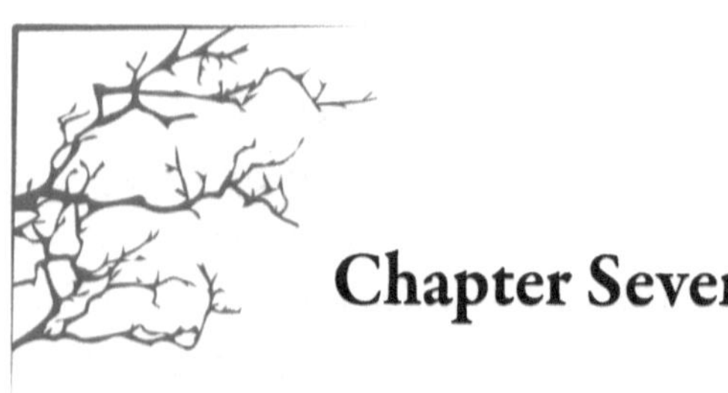

Chapter Seven

The Set-Up

The woods stared at him. If anyone had ever said those words to him, he'd have laughed and thought them to be scared little dainty creatures unable to survive a day in nature. Unless he realized they were talking about Ravenwood. Then he'd probably think them crazier than an outhouse rat for going anywhere close to that cursed property.

Yet, here he was, standing on the shoulder of Route 116 next to his car, staring into the most cursed woods on the planet. It's where he had been for over an hour trying to muster enough courage to venture into them.

'I don't have to do this.' He kicked at the gravel on the edge of the road. *'It's the stupidest idea you've ever agreed to in your life.'*

A noise caused him to lift his head and look down the empty road. A bird sat on one of the wires running down the far side of the highway. It was watching him, waiting for him to go on into the trees and get killed, so it could peck away at his corpse for a few days. That's what the bird saw when it looked at him, a free warm meal.

He screamed loudly, releasing two days' worth of nerves and frustration in one vocal rendition, and the bird fluttered away. It didn't make him feel better. In fact, it left him worse off than he was. His throat burned from the strain, and he needed a drink. The sports drink he bought at a gas station up the road was finished off before he pulled over. He'd been awful thirsty when he filled up the tank and knew he should've bought two.

'It could be faked.' He didn't have to do this here. He could go anywhere, and no one would be the wiser. Except he knew better. He'd know, and he wanted it to be the honest truth when he went back home. Besides, there's probably some way to track the location the video was taken. Everyone had sacrificed their privacy for the sake of technology. If it ever came to light that he lied about it, he'd have to leave the country to escape the lifelong harassment he'd receive.

"It wouldn't be that bad," he whispered.

'Damn it, Carla,' he slapped the hood of the car with his open hand.

He pulled a pack of Camel Menthol from his shirt pocket, squeezing one between his lips while he lit it. 'One more. Then I'm going.' It was the same thing he told himself with the last three he smoked.

Noah paced the road, muttering to himself and cussing his new bride under his breath. It had been a set up. "I was tricked!" he yelled at the road. No one was around to listen to his side of the story.

A long flume of smoke released from his mouth and nose. He should've listened to them, to all of them. Carla was bad news, only out for his money. She was using him, but no, he wouldn't listen. He grew sick of hearing everyone constantly running her down until they stopped talking to him about anything important for fear of triggering his temper.

He leaned against the car and kicked the tire with his heel.

Then he did it again harder. Again. And again. Each time he kicked it harder than the last until he swung around after kicking it, pain shooting through his foot, grunting and swearing as he did.

Another drag. The cigarette wasn't calming his nerves this time. If he didn't go into the trees now, he never would. It had to happen. It was the only way. If he died, it was almost better than the alternative.

'She wasn't even upset!'

Carla stole his heart and blinded him to her every fault. It was a monumental task considering she was made up entirely of them. He could see that now. Those who tried to warn him she was a gold digger were pushed away. He thought they were only saying that because she didn't grow up in the country club crowd and live on the trust fund side of town. She convinced him everybody in his life hated her because she was poor when really they hated her horns visible to everyone but him.

So he married her. It took him less than twenty four hours to regret saying, "I do." Forty-eight hours after the ceremony, he was psyching himself up to meet an agonizing death in the forest of no return.

He could go anywhere else to film this. He could go back now. He could slip his lawyer the evidence which would clear him in a trial. *Hopefully, it will clear me. It doesn't prove I didn't sleep with Tina only that I was set up to do so.*

When he awoke the morning after his wedding and saw Tina lying in bed next to him, it really didn't make him stop and worry. They had all stayed at the reception a little too long, enjoying themselves, dancing and making trip after trip to the free bar courtesy of his parents. He barely remembered making his way to the hotel room where they continued a little after party.

It was Tina who jumped out of bed crying. She was completely naked and kept apologizing while she searched for her clothes which were scattered everywhere. "I'm so sorry. I didn't mean for this to happen. I won't say anything. I promise. I can't believe we did this to Carla."

'Did what? The last thing I remember about that night was struggling to unlock the door to the room.'

Noah took one last drag then poised to flick the cigarette from his fingers out of habit. He paused and secretly stole a glance at the woods. He opened the car door and deposited the still burning butt into the travel ashtray between the front seats. There were some risks not worth taking.

He really hadn't thought anything had happened between them. His head pounded and his stomach churned. He could barely move let alone try to talk to her. When a half dressed Tina opened the room door to leave and found Carla asleep in the hallway still in her wedding gown with yesterday's makeup streaked down her face, that's when Noah knew his life was about to fall apart.

Noah shook his head. *'This is so stupid.'*

His hands were trembling. His heart raced. He was going to do his best, but he wasn't ignorant to the fact his death was more than likely at hand.

He took his phone from his pocket and pulled up the video option on his camera and began recording. The Route 116 sign on the far edge of the highway was where he began filming. As he panned across the road, he lifted his phone high to get the very top of the castle peering over the trees. No one was going to accuse him of not following through.

Then he held it in front of him as he walked into the woods. He moved slowly. *Each step was careful and deliberate.*

'That dumb pre-nup. I should've known.'

A few more yards passed with him delicately moving branches out of the way. He was careful not to snap any of them. The ground was scoured before he put his foot down as he moved forward, farther into the woods. There would be nothing done by him warranting punishment if he could help it.

A bird cawed overhead, and he jumped, looking up. He saw the large black bird circling him, and he swore it was the same one from the road. It was following him, ready for a banquet.

'All those years I defended her to everybody I know. I called them snobs who looked down their noses at anyone not born with a silver spoon in their mouth.'

He took a few more steps and realized the tree coverage was growing thicker. It made it appear darker like the sun was already setting. It wasn't too dark he couldn't see by what light trickled through, but dark enough to cast shadows which made him fear something might be lurking, waiting for him.

'I should've known when she came to me wanting a pre-nup. She requested it! Obviously, that was proof she wasn't only interested in my bank account.'

There were only two ways she could get a handsome sum of money. If he died within the first two years of marriage, before most life insurance policies pay in full, she'd get it all. *'I wonder why she sent me to Ravenwood.'*

If she could prove he was unfaithful, she was entitled to half. Otherwise, the amount awarded her is based on how many years they were married. The ink wasn't even dry on the marriage certificate yet which meant she got jack squat.

Lucky for him, her friend Tina didn't have the heart to go through with it. She had been a part of the plan. Set it up. Make it look like he slept with another woman on their wedding night. Brand him a cheater. It would be open and shut in front of the judge. Carla would get half of everything. Half of half would be enough for her to be set for life. Tina got cold feet and finally confessed Noah had passed out on the bed while Carla was still in the room. She claimed to not remember how or why she undressed and slept next to him, but there were no signs anything besides sleeping happened between them during the night. Carla was livid!

'I bet she never speaks to Tina again. She's still going to get a couple hundred grand, but better than half.'

He glanced at the screen on his phone. It was almost to the ten minute mark which was all he had to do, but he was going to wait a little longer since he started recording before he entered the woods. The stakes were too dire for a technicality. Every fight or flight instinct in his body was screaming at him to stop. Leave now while you still can was reverberating through his mind. He couldn't even wait where he was at for the remainder of the time. The deal was ten minutes in and ten minutes out.

'Now, here I am. Making sure she accepts my apology, realizes I never cheated on her. All because I was stupid enough to fall in love with her.'

There was a ravine ahead, so he had to walk along it. He kept a good distance from the edge. It would be too easy to slip and fall, or worse. Something could be tempted to give him a shove. It was the dangers he wasn't aware of which caused him the most worry.

Noah reached the point where he could go back and never felt more thankful. The finish line was directly ahead of him. He kept the same steady pace because he had to keep to his end of the bargain, and he didn't want to upset the trees now when he was over halfway through. He had walked halfway to his death, and he needed to walk the other half to save his life.

The ravine appeared in front of him again, and he realized he somehow got turned around. He tried not to panic. He controlled his breathing with long steady breaths. It was going to be fine. It didn't mean anything more than a couple extra minutes in the woods.

The bird was still high overhead. With the branches intertwining above him, he couldn't see it. It occasionally sounded out a call to him, letting him know he was being followed. The bird was asking him to give up already because it was hungry.

A short time later, he found the ravine again. It had been over a half an hour since he entered the woods. The camera on his phone was still recording every step he took. It was becoming harder not to lose it. The little light he had was fading, but he wasn't going to stop recording until it became too dark to see. Then he'd have to turn it off to use the flashlight. The camera had been draining his battery since he entered Ravenwood, and he hoped it held out long enough for him to get back to his car.

Noah's path met the ravine regardless of which direction he walked. There was very little light to see by, and his battery was almost dead. He thought he could do it. He'd been careful, paying attention to every move, but it wasn't enough. His final moments would be here in Ravenwood. He could only hope the lack of a body would be enough to prevent payout to Carla on the prenup.

It wasn't just one ravine, or the same spot he'd find himself. There were multiple ravines of various depths and widths, or he was just coming back to the same one at different parts of it. The walls were closing in on him too. It was taking less and less time for the ravine to appear. He had a feeling he'd soon find himself trapped in a small section of woods surrounded by deep drop offs on all sides.

Something, or someone, was behind him. He could feel the change in the atmosphere as it approached. It didn't seem evil, but there wasn't anything good about this place. Whatever it was couldn't be friendly. He turned around slowly, hoping it was his frightened overactive imagination, and nothing would be there. Almost everything his mind fathomed would be better than what he saw.

There was a beautiful woman with long dark hair in an old-fashioned plain dress standing a few feet from him. She was easily the most gorgeous woman he'd ever seen. He'd heard the stories of the lady who haunted Ravenwood. This had to be her. She was a harbinger of death, the bringer of evil. She was here to foreshadow his own demise. His heartbeat slowed, and he felt calm. There was a fear gripping him, wondering how his death would occur, mainly concerned with the amount of pain he'd feel, but there was a comfort in knowing the time had arrived. The guesswork, hope and panic were gone.

He went to turn off the recording. There was enough footage for people to put the pieces together as to what happened to him if his phone was ever recovered. His parents didn't need to see or even hear his final moments.

The lady shook her head, wanting him to keep recording. She motioned for him to follow her, and he did. The woods had ways of getting what they wanted from the unwilling, and he hoped he could leave the world as painlessly as possible. Part of him believed her only to be a figment of his imagination, but it wasn't a risk worth taking.

He followed her looking at nothing but their feet. He stepped where she did, not stirring anything else as they went. He never noticed the light growing brighter in the woods, and he didn't see the break in the trees showing the road ahead until he walked through it.

The lady had led him to his car. He lifted his phone, making sure to get it on film before stopping the video. When he turned around to thank the lady, she was gone. He wondered how she knew the video was important, or if she was aware of just how much was riding on it.

Noah practically ran to his car, leaving the area before the lady of the woods had a chance to change her mind. He didn't feel safe until he was back in Boston. Even then, safe wasn't the right word. It would take years before he could relax, not worrying that every bump in the night was the lady returning for him. There were still days when a crippling terror seized him, and he believed it could still happen.

His new bride was surprised to see him when he knocked on the hotel suite door. They were supposed to check out tomorrow to leave on their honeymoon. Her shock was quickly replaced with accusations that he backed out and didn't go to Ravenwood. The video set her straight. They and a few friends watched it in its entirety. It was something Noah would always regret. There were voices on it he didn't hear while he was there.

"Run!" One voice tried to warn him. Most of them begged him. "Help me!" There were so many different voices. Many of them mere murmurs in the background which couldn't be deciphered or laughter. They were laughing at him.

Carla was so happy after watching the video. "You really do love me!" she gushed. She threw her arms around him, and covered his face with gentle pecks, putting on a show for her friends. She tried to plant a firm kiss on his lips, but he refused to kiss her back. "We can be together again."

This was her nonnegotiable offer. If he loved her like he claimed he did, he would go to Ravenwood to prove it. The woods didn't harm the innocent. *But it's not their past actions the woods judge.* Noah knew this, but many didn't. *It's how you act in their presence.*

His wife insisted if he loved her and had been faithful, he could walk ten minutes into the woods and back out without being hurt. It was a test to prove himself to her.

He pushed her away and stood up. "I want a divorce," he said. It would be worth the small payout to get rid of her. It disgusted him how she tried to set him up for money, and he was livid over the act she was putting on for those around them now.

"But you went to Ravenwood," she said in shock. Her eyes lowered and darted back and forth. She was probably trying to remember how much money she would receive for a forty-eight hour sham of a marriage.

"That's right," Noah said.

Carla glanced at her friends. No one's eyes would meet

hers. Many had small smiles on their lips. They were enjoying the show even though they would comfort her and bad mouth him when he left. "I don't understand. Why then?"

"I went into the woods because I'd rather die than be married to you for one more minute," Noah spat and left the hotel room.

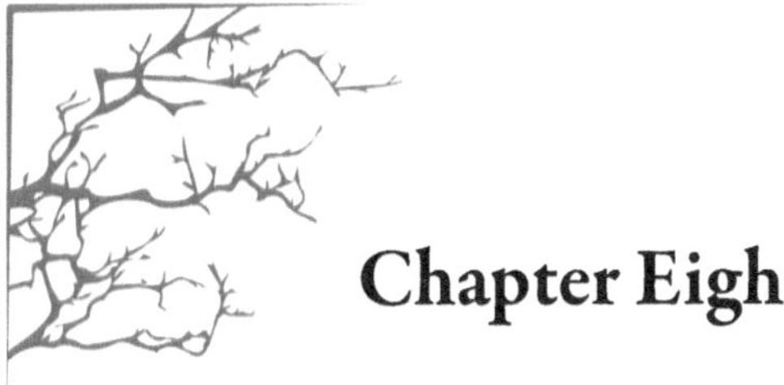

Chapter Eight

Face Your Fears

Her eyes flew open, and she immediately felt better even though she was still shrouded in darkness, unable to see more than shadows. It was the shadows which terrified her most. Her breathing, while still hard and deep, wasn't as difficult as it had been. Her skin covered in a cold, clammy sweat, but not as cold as the air in the woods at night.

It took several moments for her to get her bearings. She was in her bedroom. She was in Lemon Grove. She was safe.

Mandy could see her window, her dresser, the pillow next to her on the other side of the bed, the door to her closet, and the footboard. She could touch her nightstand as well as her phone laying on it, her blanket, and her mattress. She could hear the traffic outside, the hum of her refrigerator drifting down the hallway, and someone talking in the parking lot. She could smell the vanilla scented air freshener which sprayed on a timer and the remnants of the perfume she'd wore earlier that day. There was nothing to taste, not without getting out of bed, and she wasn't ready to take that leap.

'But why is it dark?'

She reached for the cell phone on the nightstand and turned on the flashlight, shining it along the wall. The nightlight was still plugged into the outlet, but the bulb had burned out. She sat up and threw her legs over the side of the bed.

There's no going back to sleep easily after a dream like that. She would know. She'd been having them for nearly twenty years, ever since the woods took the lives of her friends.

Taking the nightlight, she walked around to the other side of her bed. The other nightlight she used was still plugged in and burned out as well. *'That's strange,'* she thought. She bought them on the same day and used them every night, but they had never burned out at the same time. The hairs on the back of her neck stood on end, and she could feel the goosebumps like clattering clay tiles being laid as they traveled up her arm. She wondered what might be lurking in the darkest corners of her room, wondering if Ravenwood had finally found her.

There was a flash, and the room lit up. The darkness invaded once again quickly. *'Lightening. The weatherman might actually be right for once.'*

Mandy brought the nightlights down a hallway lit up by a third one matching the two she carried. The outlet was installed just for that purpose. The light over the stove welcomed her into the kitchen, and she set the nightlights on the counter. Several packages of replacement bulbs were stored in the first cabinet.

She had finished off the last roll of toilet paper because she didn't know it was the last one when she went to the store. She ran out of dryer sheets often. Many mornings there was no milk for her cereal because she forgot to stop by the market on her way home from work. The one thing she never ran out of was bulbs for the seven nightlights in her home.

She took them back to her bedroom, flipping the switch

on the wall as she entered. After plugging them back in and turning them on, she left her room, switching the light back off. She wouldn't return to her bedroom before morning. Having them on overnight was habit. They were part of her routine, and routine was the only thing keeping her resembling sanity.

In the living room, she lifted the top of the coffee table, revealing the storage compartment underneath and pulled out the pillow and blanket she kept there just in case. She wasn't fooling anyone.

That's what she told people anyway. "Just in case someone crashes here for the night. Just in case I want to cuddle up on the couch and watch old movies when I'm sick." The reality of it was they were used weekly, sometimes nightly.

This was the compromise she made with her therapist. Bedrooms are for relaxing. They are for rest. They are for sleep. There shouldn't be a television set, but the light and the noises helps her. The ghosts who haunt her won't attack if someone else is talking even if it's an actor on the screen. It may be a childish belief, but she holds fast to it. She begins every night in her bedroom, and she ends most of them on the couch.

Face your fears.

She made herself comfortable and put on a movie she loved. It was a movie she'd watched a thousand times. It was one she could easily fall asleep while watching without struggling to keep her eyes open, wanting to know what happened next. It was an upbeat comedy. She hadn't been able to watch horror flicks since her senior year of high school.

At some point before dawn after she began the third movie on her nightmare playlist, exhaustion overtook her. She awoke to the sound of her alarm with daylight flooding through the window.

She folded the blanket and stored it with the pillow then began her day. She showered, dressed, and made her bed. The nightlights were switched off beginning with the ones in her room. She went back into the bathroom to turn off the third then the one in the hallway; number four, her so called office housed the fifth, into the pantry; six, and in the living room; seven. Finally she made her way to the kitchen where she turned off the light over the stove. *'Eight,'* she thought.

That was the order. It was how she turned them off. They were switched on in reverse every afternoon long before dusk rolled around, not giving pure darkness a chance to invade. The only rooms without nightlights were the closets and the spare bedroom. It would be a spare bedroom anyway if it had a bed. If she needed anything from those rooms after sunset, it would have to wait until the morning.

Breakfast was oatmeal because it was Saturday. During the week, she had cereal. Tomorrow she would cook.

She dumped the morning's doses from the pill organizer into her hand and swallowed them with a drink of water. The glass she sat upside down on the mat next to the sink. She carried her oatmeal and coffee to the table to eat.

After breakfast, she grabbed her purse and hesitated before picking up her already prepared backpack waiting by the front door. It's Saturday. Today she goes hiking. It's her least favorite day of the week. The rain had stopped during the night. The ground was soft, but not too muddy. Even Mandy didn't buy it as an excuse to stay home.

"Face your fears." It's her therapist's voice in her head. The thing her therapist didn't understand was anything waiting for her on these trails in southern California which could hurt her was nothing compared to what she narrowly escaped at Ravenwood.

'All because of a stupid head injury.'

Mandy had tripped and knocked herself out cold. If it weren't for that, she would've met the same fate as her friends. It's funny how death changed her perception. Even twenty years later, she can remember the teasing. The extra baby weight she carried was what they joked about most. Looking back on it now, it was all in good fun. In her memories, she laughed along with them. She didn't quite remember accurately how hurtful their comments had been and how much she wanted to shy away from spending time with them because of it. Twenty years later, she considered them the best friends she ever had, and she would give anything to bring them back.

She suffered a concussion and a blown ear drum on the left side. It's what the doctors attributed to the voices she heard. They were hallucinations brought on by head injury. A couple days were spent in the hospital for observation and to receive fluids for dehydration. She was let off with a warning while her friends didn't make it out of the woods alive.

The drive to Iron Mountain Peak wasn't very long. The trail was over five miles. It wasn't the hardest hike in her rotation, but it was one of the more strenuous ones. This was her Saturday morning routine. Every weekend she went into nature in an attempt to conquer her fears because her therapist believed it would help her get better.

Mandy was on autopilot. It could've been thinking about how her fears lived across the country, but she thought about those fears every day of her life since spring break her senior year. It could've been the new medication her doctor had put her on for anxiety, but she would've expected any side effects to appear by now.

She was in her own little world when she pulled into the airport and booked the first flight to Albany. There were two changeovers along the way. Luckily for Ravenwood, she wouldn't have to wait long. It wasn't until it was announced passengers needed to return to their seats and fasten their seatbelts because the plane would be landing soon on the third flight that she snapped out of it. Clear across country, soaring through the clouds, she realized where she was going. It could've been many things causing her to get on the plane that day, but Mandy knew it was Ravenwood beckoning her to return.

Anyone else would've stayed at the airport and booked a flight home. They'd have scolded themselves for the waste of money while simultaneously freaking out over what kind of psychotic break must have caused this behavior. Not Mandy.

Face your fears.

This had been a long time coming. It was something she had thought about at least once every day since she saw the dark colored bags on the side of the road and realized her friends were inside of them. She should've been lying there with them.

There was a change of clothes in her backpack. She was always prepared when she left the house for a hike. She'd never needed them until now, but she packed them week after week, just in case. She went to the rental car counter and drove herself straight to Appleton where she stayed for the night.

The panic didn't take over until she was checked in to the motel. Everything she really needed was still at home. All of her medications were in the pill organizer on the shelf in the kitchen. She'd already missed taking them at noon and with dinner. There were no pills for that night or the next day either. Most importantly, there were no nightlights.

Strangely, the idea of visiting Ravenwood gave her a sense of peace. There was a stillness in understanding she was exactly where she was supposed to be. She imagined it was similar to anyone who accepted a terminal prognosis from a doctor. This was it. Nothing could be done to change it and fighting it only aggravated the situation.

She tried to stick to the agreement. The light in the bathroom was left on with the door cracked several inches, flooding the room enough to chase away the shadows. It wasn't enough. The curtains were thin. Every time she opened her eyes, she could see trees. Ravenwood or not, they appeared to be moving closer to her each time she checked. The television was left on, playing infomercials all night. The worst it could do was give her nightmares about absorbent towels or the latest breakthrough in acne treatments.

The next morning when she left her room she skipped the continental breakfast and went to a restaurant. It was Sunday. That meant a hot breakfast. She wasn't going to have her last meal be a cheese danish and three hour old coffee. It was a difficult choice, and she took far too long to order. In the end, she got all three: pancakes, french toast and an omelet. It was fitting to have all her favorites one last time.

When she walked to her car parked near the edge of the lot after eating, she noticed a long stick lying in the grass. She picked it up and studied it. The length and sturdiness of it was perfect for a walking stick as if someone left it there for her intentionally. She tossed it in the car and used the GPS to travel out of Appleton down 116.

Mandy recognized the area where she pulled off on the side of the road. She was certain some would argue after two decades it wouldn't be possible. Some things had changed. The ditch on the side of the road had been freshly mowed. The road itself looked no worse for wear than when she'd come here with her friends back in high school. The trees had grown larger, and one lay haphazardly toppled on its neighbor. There was a fleeting feeling of sadness, an ache from the loss of it.

Before she left the car, she wrote a note, laying it on the passenger seat. It could take days for an abandoned vehicle to be reported in these parts, if not weeks, but she wanted to help whoever responded to the call. She signed her name and dated it.

On March 28, 1986, four friends entered Ravenwood. I was the only one who made it out alive. Today I've returned to let the woods finish what they started.

With her bag on her back and walking stick in hand, Mandy walked through the tree line. Once inside the property, she froze. Part of her wanted to turn around, reassuring herself she could still see the road and her car. Part of her didn't want to turn her back on the woods.

For a long time, she stayed right there not moving, thinking this would be sufficient. She was here.

Face your fears.

It was the most absurd and direct way imaginable, but she was doing it. Almost. She knew it wouldn't be enough.

Putting one trembling leg in front of the other, she moved forward slowly. The terrain wasn't impassable. It wasn't nearly as overgrown as what she had walked through after waking up on the ground as a teenager. She walked until she was lost.

She found a clear patch of grass and sat down to wait. Nothing happened. Nothing came for her. She lay down on her back and watched the branches of the trees sway gently in the breeze. It was beautiful here.

A homesick feeling grew in the pit of her stomach. Mandy had spent her entire life trying to put Ravenwood as far behind her as she could. It never occurred to her how much she missed home.

"Yes, autumn out east is beautiful." She would unbelievingly tell new people whenever they learned where she was from. Laying there in the cold grass she found herself wishing it was autumn. She longed to see the vivid colors paint a portrait across the landscape once more.

Her memories told her it hadn't taken near this long for the trees to come for her friends. The doctors had been saying her memories were faulty due to her head injury ever since that day.

The sun traveled in the sky overhead. The slight chill she'd been experiencing was warmed by the rays falling directly on her through the branches above her. She never wore her watch while hiking because it distracted her from what she was doing. It created a constraint, an excuse. Time forced her to want to go home because other things required her attention. That's why she didn't have her watch when she made this spontaneous trip. The sun was her only time piece.

It wouldn't be long before she began to question what she was doing and if she should leave. Boredom, if nothing else, would've driven her out of the woods. If only it had come a little sooner.

"Maaaaannnnddddyyyy."

She jolted to her feet and spun around. There was no one there. *'Keep the sun to your left.'*

"Where'd that thought come from?" she wondered out loud. It was over head. The sun wouldn't guide her back to the road.

"Help me, Mandy."

Her eyes widened, and her mouth fell open. "Erin?" Her voice was barely above a whisper. She hadn't heard her voice in two decades except in the nightmares where Erin haunted her.

"Mandy! Where are you?"

The little hairs stood on the back of her neck, and a chill ran down her spine. Claire's voice was behind her, but she didn't dare look to see if anyone, or anything, was there.

There was scattered giggling. It came from the trees then would ring directly by her ear. From every direction, she could hear her friends' teasing laughter. The trees began to sway, and she didn't have time to realize it was her who was spinning.

The ground came at her fast, too fast to brace herself. When she opened her eyes, it was like she was eighteen again, in the same position as when she came to in high school. She rolled onto her back and listened. The voices were gone.

Mandy opened her eyes and screamed. The faces of all three of them hovered over them. Erin, Claire, and Missy were unaged, but barely recognizable. They were covered in wounds, still bleeding, cuts and gashes, pale skin peppered with deep bruises.

A twig snapped behind her head, and the faces vanished,

if they had ever been there at all. Mandy stood up as quickly as she could manage. Her head pounded, and she felt weak, dizzy. When she turned in the direction of the noise, her vision blurred, and she squeezed her eyes shut several times trying to clear it. Something was there, and it was coming toward her. All she could make out was a darkened figure.

As it came into focus, Mandy saw it was a beautiful young woman with flowing black hair. Her dress was dated, a period piece. This was the rumored lady who made the woods her home.

"Amanda Sullivan," the lady said.

'How? No one calls me Amanda.'

The lady placed her hand on Mandy's shoulder, guiding her forward and walked along side of her. "I've been waiting for you."

Mandy walked in step with her. The lady took her time, making her way through the trees like a Sunday stroll in the park. They didn't speak, and Mandy's heart thudded against her chest, vibrating in her ears. It was coming although she didn't know exactly when or how, but this was it.

The sight of her car in the distance along the road caused her to gasp. The lady was gone. Mandy spun around, but she had disappeared.

She ran out of the woods, across the road, and stood on the tips of her toes to see the very tops of the castle through the trees. They hadn't spoken, but the knowledge the lady gave her was clear. It was time to go home and wait.

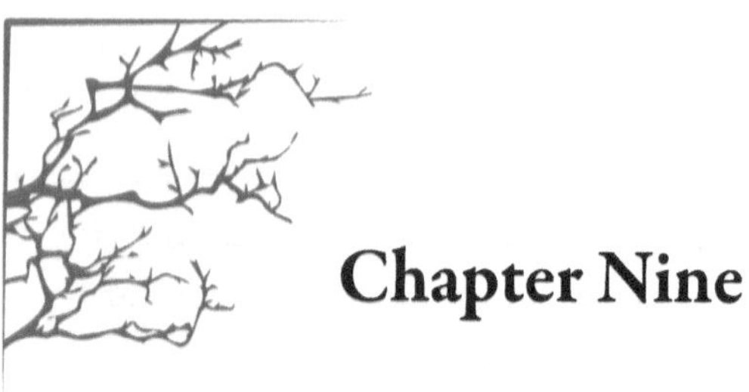

Chapter Nine

Twins

Given how long the pregnancy lasted, Joseph and Rozalia were oddly unprepared for child birth. Had her labors begun shortly after arriving in America, they would've been ready. If their child had been born shortly after they emerged from the woods, they would've been more than equipped. They were expecting it. After another full winter of carrying the child they conceived a decade before in another country in what was to them another time, another life, they almost believed the child would never come into the world.

Long gone were the days when they dropped everything over every little ache or pain in Rozalia's midsection or back thinking the time had finally arrived. The pregnancy was permanent. As strange as it was to think, it's what both of them believed. The idea lingered in the back of their minds, nagging at them from time to time whenever it forced its way through to the forefront of their thoughts. At any rate, the child was going to arrive on her own schedule regardless of what nature or science dictated.

Both of them felt shunned when they first arrived, but it was nothing compared to the isolation after they returned from their trek in the woods. People avoided them at all costs until the day a group of men turned up unexpectedly to meet the couple and welcome them to the area. Joseph wasn't blind to what was really going on. They were curious, wanting to see what was happening, wondering about the near constant stream of shipments driving through town during the autumn past. Still he was ecstatic to have guests to show off the castle. He'd have entertained them longer if their baby hadn't picked that moment to make her debut.

Rozalia, ever the cool head, remained in the grand hall, working through each contraction as the pain returned. Joseph ran through their home, grabbing everything he thought they might need, leaving the carefully packed bag Rozalia had prepared months ago sitting in their bedroom. The bag he brought to the hospital was never used, nor could it have been. Weeks after they came home, Rozalia noticed it in the corner and set about unpacking it.

The bag looked like it had been thrown together by a child off to a play date with his imagination. It contained two of her blouses, but no other clothing. There was the comb Joseph used and had complained for several days he couldn't find before purchasing a replacement. He also brought a picture of the two of them from their wedding day, three spoons, a kitchen towel, and a candlestick.

'Whatever did he expect to happen during my labors?' It would be a funny story to share amongst friends if she had any besides her husband.

A home birth was out of the question. It was what Rozalia wanted, what she preferred. It was how their child would've been born in her home country. No doctor, nurse, midwife, or even just a woman who was a mother herself experienced in childbirth, would step foot inside the inn to help them deliver.

As much as the tales of the property had begun to brew long before the land was gifted to Joseph from his parents, it was Rozalia herself who frightened them.

Rozalia would've attempted the birth on her own. She had attended to several in Europe. She had been there for two of her sister's labors, helped her mother with her youngest brothers delivery, and three of her friends who had married before the war. There wasn't a crack in her confidence she could've guided Joseph through the process, but this pregnancy was far from normal. Deep down she worried about their baby and believed it best to deliver with at least a doctor on hand.

They loaded in the car finally, and Joseph drove them to the hospital. It wasn't customary for the father to be with his wife during labor. Neither Joseph nor his wife cared about what people considered normal, or if they'd be thought strange. The hospital wouldn't allow it. "Husbands only get in the way," one nurse told him. They forced Rozalia to give birth alone with only strangers in the room.

Joseph remained in the hallway, pacing back and forth by the door, listening to his wife's pained screams, listening to her call out his name and being unable to go to her. After forcing his way into the room several times, he was warned. "If you come in here again, we will have you removed from the premises."

It felt like an eternity before the screaming stopped, and the soft cries of a newborn drifted through the door to his ears. Joseph relaxed sitting on a bench in the hall. His head dropped, and a smile radiated across his face. It was his daughter. He didn't need the nurse to inform him what the lady already foretold. It was his little Nikolett.

It wasn't until his relief washed over him he noticed another man farther down the hallway. His head was hung as Joseph's had been, but it wasn't from a blissful surrender of contentment. It was sorrow.

A nurse emerged from Rozalia's room and glanced at Joseph briefly. He opened his mouth to ask if he could see her and his child. The nurse scurried away panicked.

Joseph stood and took a step toward the door, wondering if he should enter. Several people appeared in the hall running toward Rozalia's room. "It won't be much longer," the last one said, before disappearing through the door.

His pacing resumed. He could hear the frantic tone of the voices even if he couldn't make out the words. *'What's wrong? Something is wrong.'*

All of the fears he had throughout the entire pregnancy returned. It wasn't safe carrying a child for so long. There were bound to be complications. Something was wrong with their child. He was certain of it. Images popped into his head of how Nikolett might look. He had feared their child would only be part human and part demon. She was a demon like what was in the woods which controlled his land.

When someone did come out of the room to speak to him, he only caught pieces and phrases of what was being said. It was too much to comprehend at once.

"Lost a lot of blood."

"Unconscious."

"Had to help the second child."

"Resting comfortably."

"Both babies are doing well."

"We'll let you know when you can see her," the nurse said.

Joseph's head was spinning. It wasn't his head, but the room. It swayed and rocked around him. Sitting on the bench, he felt like he needed to lay down. He gripped the seat of the bench for support to remain upright.

"Are you okay?" the voice echoed. The woman speaking to him appeared to be standing at the far end of the tunnel and moving farther away.

His stomach heaved, and he gasped for air. With one final spin, he closed his eyes. When he opened them again, he was on the floor. His nose was on fire, burning from whatever was used to awaken him.

The nurse who had been talking to him was standing over him, asking if he was alright. Remarkably, he felt much better. She helped him sit up, leaning his back against the bench, calling for help to lift him.

"I'm fine," Joseph assured her. "I just need to sit here a minute."

The nurse nodded.

Joseph glanced back at the man down the hall. The stranger was unfazed by the commotion being carried out a short distance from him. "You said babies?" He questioned the nurse.

"That's right," she smiled. "Twins. Both girls. Darling, beautiful little angels."

'Angels,' he thought. Joseph wondered if she chose that word specifically to ease the fears he must surely have, or if it was an innocent remark made by someone who didn't know the full depth of their history.

All these months, all this worry he had twisting around inside him over this child. A baby was supposed to be a blessing, and it was. She was. Their baby girl was going to make them a family and add to their lives in ways they couldn't yet comprehend. Then, there was the woods to consider. The lady and the way she controlled them. Their very existence rested in her hands. Bringing a baby into that world wasn't what they signed up for when Rozalia became pregnant, and now, he learned he brought two into it.

"That man," Joseph said softly.

"I'm sorry. I didn't hear you," the nurse said. "What was that?"

Joseph stood and politely shooed the nurse's hands away when she attempted to help. He was fine. The news just shook him a bit when it first struck.

"The man down the hall," Joseph said, trying to nod discreetly in his direction. "What happened there?"

"Oh," the nurse said sadly. "Yes, his child was stillborn."

He looked at the nurse quickly and back at the man. "The baby was..."

"Born asleep, yes," the nurse finished for him. "Beautiful girl too." The nurse cleared her throat. "Would you like to see yours?"

"I thought I couldn't."

"Your wife is resting, but your babies will be in the nursery soon," she explained. "Why don't you visit the cafeteria? Get some strength back in you, and I'll meet you there afterward. Show you the two precious angels."

Joseph nodded even though he didn't feel like eating. It was better than sitting in the hallway bored and agitated waiting to see Rozalia. It was far better than wishing his fortune hadn't been doubled when there was a man not far from him living a nightmare.

He'd never admit it to the nurse, but he felt like a different man after having a hot meal. The man was no longer in the hallway when he came back through which eased some of the guilt off Joseph's shoulders. He found his way to the nursery and stood in the window looking at the half dozen or so babies, guessing which were his when the nurse spied him.

The nurse pointed out the two little girls on the other side of the glass. They were quiet, resting soundly, while the babies surrounding them were crying. One had a headful of black hair with features easily the carbon copy of his wife. The other had a tuft of lighter color hair and his nose. They weren't going to be identical which could be a blessing in disguise itself.

The nurse walked through the side door and joined him in the hall. "How's my wife?" he asked, not taking his eyes off his two baby girls.

"She's still resting. She's going to be fine. You'll be able to see her soon."

"Which is which?" he asked, pointing to the girls.

"The one with the hair is the oldest," the nurse beamed.

"Nikolett," he said with a smile. She should be as beautiful as her mother.

The idea had come to him while he ate. Most people say to sleep on it. Things will be clearer in the morning. He'd always found a full stomach helped him think. Joseph knew what he had to do. He just hoped Rozalia never found out.

"Listen," he said, staring at the babies. "This is what I want to do."

The nurse was appalled at his suggestion. She laughed nervously thinking he couldn't be serious, or it must still be the shock of the day's events wearing him thin. She tried to get him to sit a spell, discuss it with Rozalia first, or at least wait until morning before making a decision this big.

Joseph was adamant about what he wanted to do. Not a word of it was to ever fall onto Rozalia's ears either. As her husband, it was his decision, and it was up to him how much she was told.

The lady might come after him for it, and that was a chance he was willing to take. He trusted in what he knew about her enough to accept she'd never harm a child. The babies would grow up healthy and well. This was the only way one of them would have a chance at a normal life. He'd do it for them both if it wouldn't break Rozalia's heart. It was already breaking his.

Rozalia's eyes fluttered open several times before she began to get her bearings. She looked around the room, seeing the nurse, and it alarmed her. The light coming through the window was brighter than when she had delivered, and there was no baby in sight. When she saw Joseph, the panic really set in, and she tried to sit up.

The nurse flew to her side, stopping her from moving too much. "Rest now. You've been through quite a bit in the last twenty-four hours."

"Twenty-four... What day is it?" She asked Joseph. Her eyes widened in fear. "The baby! Where is she?" She frantically looked around for the basinet which was in the nursery.

"If you're going to cause this much agitation, perhaps its best you leave," the nurse told him coldly.

"You and I both know she's agitated because she hasn't seen her *child*." He stressed the singularity of the word. "It has nothing to do with me."

Joseph and that woman had been at odds since they spoke at the nursery the night Rozalia gave birth. She'd love to have a moment alone with his wife to plant a seed in her mind, but he wouldn't give her the chance. If she found a way to do it anyhow, he'd have her job stripped from her so fast she'd get whiplash from them yanking that funny hat off her head.

He sat on the edge of Rozalia's bed and took her hand in his, lifting it to his lips and kissing the back of it. "Shh, my dear," he told her. "Everything is fine. Our little Nikolett is fine."

The nurse snorted and stomped out of the room. Joseph ignored her, but he caught Rozalia watching her with curiosity as she left.

"Is something wrong?" she asked.

"Not anymore," he smiled. He explained to her there were a few complications, but everything had worked out fine. She'd be home in no time with a beautiful baby to tend.

"Nikolett." The name rolled off her tongue in her accented English. "You named her?"

Joseph nodded. "Nikolett Pataki Weaver," he beamed. The middle name was supposed to be Margaret after his wife, but life had other plans.

"What made you change it?"

He shrugged knowing his wife could never learn the real reason. "It had a better ring to it." That lie was easy to tell because it was the truth. He'd have named their child Margaret like they had agreed if there had been only one.

"Nikolett Pataki." She tested the sound of it a few times. "I do like it."

Joseph breathed a sigh of relief. It wouldn't have hurt to

keep the name as it was supposed to be. It was an impulse to divide it between the girls.

The nurse returned pushing the basinet. Rozalia peered as much as she could but wasn't able to see their baby without sitting up. It was something the nurse still insisted she not do. She reached into the basinet and carried the baby to Rozalia, giving Joseph a look that ordered him to move. She laid Nikolett carefully onto the bed next to Rozalia who curled up around her.

Tears crept down his wife's face. Tears of pure joy from seeing their child for the first time. Seeing the two of them together, he'd never felt more love overflow from his chest, and he hadn't known he was capable of such an extreme feeling as this. He'd do everything he could to keep his family safe, and he believed he'd already proven that in the most severe way imaginable.

Her complications were going to keep in the hospital for a few days, and Joseph settled in to stay with her. It didn't please the nurse she wouldn't get rid of him anytime soon. Whenever Rozalia was watching, he'd shoot the nurse a look reminding her she was there to do a job, not butt into people's business.

Having no family close by, not that any of them would care to stop by even if they were near, one of the nuns from the hospital chapel promised to bring a few items for his unexpected stay. That night he and his wife enjoyed some homemade soup while the rest of the mothers on the floor ate whatever the kitchen sent to their room.

There was a knock at the door, and both of them wondered who might be visiting. "Come in," Joseph called out without thinking.

When the door opened, he saw Clarence, the man from the hallway. He was pushing his wife in a wheelchair. Their new baby rested peacefully in her arms.

Joseph shot out of the chair and went quickly to the door, ushering them away before his wife had a chance to see any resemblance of his features in the face of their baby.

"Thought you might like to see Margaret before we leave," Clarence said.

That he did. He wanted to hold her, to kiss her round rosy cheeks, to beg her forgiveness, but all he could do was look.

"Margaret?" Rozalia asked from her bed.

"That's right," Clarence looked knowingly at Joseph. "Margaret Ann Sullivan."

"You have a beautiful family," Joseph told him.

Clarence's wife couldn't speak for the tears flowing down her face, and the lump in her throat. All she could do was mouth the words, "Thank you."

Joseph nodded at her and took a step back in the room. "Good luck to you and your family," he said.

"Thank you." Clarence said for at least the hundredth time since they met as Joseph closed the door.

He walked back to the chair near his wife's bed and sat down.

"Margaret," she said again. "What a coincidence."

"Indeed," he agreed nervously.

"Well that explains it then."

Joseph wasn't sure what she was talking about. "Explains what?"

"When I was out after having Nikolett, I had a series of strange dreams."

"Oh?" he remarked.

"About having twins," she said, closing her eyes and getting ready to fall asleep again. "Two girls: Nikolett and Margaret."

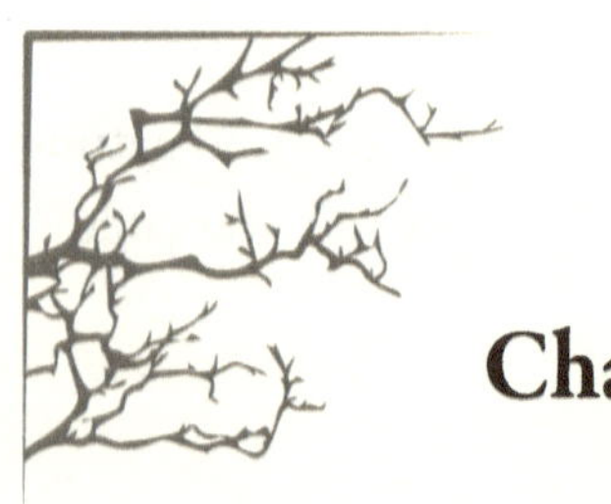

Chapter Ten

Witchcraft

No one ever believed her. Why would they? People would be skeptical of anyone who claimed to have been in the woods at Ravenwood once and lived to tell the tale, but fourteen times was a guaranteed nope.

Yet that's exactly what Celeste had done. Her first trip to Ravenwood she was as skeptic of the lore surrounding the area as people were of her claims she made frequent visits now. Had anybody disappeared there? Died there? Been injured there? Of course they had.

There probably isn't a piece of land that size in this country where no one has lost a life. Any adventurous person takes the chance when they explore. People get lost in the woods, fall down ravines, or slip while scaling a cliff all the time.

After her first trip out that way, most believed she had actually done it. They revered her. Some were in awe, clinging to her like she was experiencing her fifteen minutes of fame in the hopes it might rub off on them. Others alienated themselves from her out of fear she had been cursed and would bring evil to them if they ventured too close.

That's when she started to do the digging into the property. The stories found on reputable sources online only mentioned the deaths, the disappearances, the accidents. They listed the facts. This person went missing. This person hadn't been seen since leaving Appleton. A body was found near the road.

It's the other websites who boasted the legends. They were the ones who cater to the interests ranging across the supernatural, the mysterious, the spooky, and the things that go bump in the night. Those were the sources that filled in the blanks about the cursed land and the creepy lady of the woods.

Celeste decided to do some digging of her own. She made a weekend trip to Appleton interviewing locals claiming to be working on a research paper for college about folklore. Most were tight lipped. They'd been put through the wringer before. They weren't strangers to having their words twisted, being used to someone's advantage. There were a few who loved the sound of their own voice and chatted endlessly about Ravenwood.

Everyone had said she was lucky to have made it out alive. She should never go back again because it was tempting fate. If what the locals had to say had any truth to it, luck had nothing to do with it.

Celeste was a witch, a kitchen witch, but nonetheless a witch. She respected nature. It was the elements of nature she called upon for her spell work. When she went in to Ravenwood, she brought everything she needed and took it all with her when she left.

It was natural for her to be interested in witchcraft having been born in Salem to parents who named her Celeste. It was like they were choosing her future for her. Ravenwood seemed like a quiet spot off the beaten path where she might not be harassed for trespassing. That's why she chose it. She needed more kick to her magic than her kitchen table provided.

There was one man in Appleton named Hank. He had a lot of stories to share, enough she considered writing them all down in a book someday, with his permission of course. He was the one who explained it best. The trees simply wanted to be left alone. The source of their power was anyone's guess. Which came first? The lady of the woods? Or the woods themselves?

No one really could say for sure if the lady ruled the trees or if the trees controlled her. There was one thing he was certain about. "They won't bother you if you don't bother them."

"Have you ever gone into the woods yourself?" she asked.

"Ah, heck no," he smiled. "I might've been born naked, but it wasn't last night."

"If you're sure the trees won't mess with you, why haven't you gone?"

"Because the slightest misstep is all it takes," he said. "If I trip and fall, break a branch on my way down, I'll never see my home again. That's it. Done for. Not worth the risk."

"Round these parts, you can contribute your longevity to three things: hereditary, what you put in your body, and staying the hell out of those woods," he added.

Up until she went to Ravenwood, her spells had been met with average success. They really did nothing more than put confidence and good vibes into the universe. Meeting the day with a smile will ensure a better day than waking up dreading it.

Whenever she cast a spell, she waited for the signs it had worked. She always found them because she was looking for them. There were probably just as many signs, if not more, that it hadn't been successful. She wasn't looking for those signs though.

The spells she cast in Ravenwood were met with results like nothing she had ever experienced. That's why she went back. That's why she would continue to go back.

She didn't cast spells to ask for good grades. She knew how magic worked. Instead, she did spell work to help her understand the material better and learn. That's what raised her grade point average. There weren't spells for a winning lottery ticket. The spells were to help her and her family make smarter choices to better them financially.

Her dad announced at dinner one evening he decided after working for the same company for twenty-two years, he was going to risk it all by taking a job at a new company which recently moved nearby. He had applied on a whim. The site was on his drive to work, and he saw the signs every day.

"What?" her mom shrieked. "You didn't think to include me in this conversation?"

Her mom's anger subsided once her dad explained he'd be doubling his current salary.

All Celeste did was ask her dad one simple question. "What made you decide to apply?"

He had zero knowledge about the spell she had cast for them. "That's the thing. I can't really say what it was. I drove by the building one day while the crews were there, gutting it, and working on the remodel. There was a temporary fence on the sidewalk for people's safety with a banner hanging on it, "Coming Soon."

"For weeks, I barely glanced at it. That day was different. I saw it and thought I'm going to work there as though it had already been decided."

"That was it?" Celeste asked.

"Yeah, I couldn't get it out of my head. I looked the company up online. Seemed like a stable business branching out to the east coast. I created a resume for the first time in my life. Went on the website and applied. They called me later that day."

It was a surprise to everyone, save for Celeste, when she went back. That's the thing about witches. Spells are worked to increase the power of the magic. An energy source like Ravenwood can't be ignored once found.

After a while, they stopped believing her altogether. She invited them to come along. "I'll prove it to you."

No one took her up on the offer except for her boyfriend Lucas. They wouldn't even wait in the car on the side of Route 116. It was too close for their comfort. Most thought she was lying, but just in case she wasn't, none of them wanted to be the one questioned by police when she didn't return from the woods.

"Aren't you afraid?" they asked.

"Do you have a death wish?"

Celeste would laugh at them. "No, I just know how to work the system."

Lucas didn't buy into the hype either. He was from Seattle, and the scariest thing he'd ever seen was the grunge scene as it emerged. The stories were cool, and he loved hearing them. That's all they were: stories.

It was Celeste's witchcraft he was concerned about more than anything. He didn't want any woman of his dancing naked under a full moon whether she was alone or not. She swore it wasn't like that, but he'd seen the movies. Besides, witches lie, don't they?

He accompanied her on her fifteenth trip to Ravenwood. He had a camera ready to go to prove to his friends he had the guts to do it. This was how legends were made, and people were going to remember his name. The pint of whiskey in his jacket was kept from Celeste. She didn't care much for drinking, but he didn't think he could get through a night of witchy nonsense without it.

The first few steps into the woods were easy, but it changed somehow. He told himself it was paranoia brought on by all the rumors about the place. They'd seeped deep into his subconscious and were preying on his fears. It wasn't that the trees were actually affecting him, couldn't be.

It felt like someone was watching him, coming closer with every step he took. Celeste had warned him to be careful about where he walked, but he couldn't think about that now. His eyes were glued to the woods, searching for whatever it was that was about to attack.

They passed so many places she could've set up her junk. Each time he pointed an area out, she said, "No, we're almost there."

Almost was still a twenty minute hike away. The bottle stashed in the inside pocket of his jacket was the only thing keeping him from bolting from the woods with his tail between his legs. He was behind her, so the first few swigs were secret. When she stopped to look at her hand drawn map, he stupidly stole a kiss, and she could taste the alcohol on him. He thought for sure the rest of the night would be a screaming match.

"We're not going to fight. Not now. Not here," she told him.

'Thank God for small miracles.' He was doing a happy dance on the inside.

"We'll talk about this later."

'Talk? Yeah, right,' he took another sip. There was no need hiding it any longer. The cat was already out of the bag.

It was boring watching her unpack the two bags she dragged through the woods with her. Well, one she lugged around plus the one he wore on his back. He offered to help. This place gave him the creeps. The hairs on his neck were constantly on end, and the goose bumps on his arms never went away. She refused him every time.

There was a method to it. He didn't practice the craft, so he wouldn't understand. *'Practice,'* he scoffed. *'More like playing with expensive toys.'*

He took her to a new age shop for her birthday. There wasn't a candle in the store for less than five bucks. A pack of twelve was less than that at any corner market. The biggest rip off scam in history were these places catering to emotionally vulnerable women so desperate to find true love they'd try anything.

By the time she was ready to start, the bottle was empty. In hind sight, if he had the chance to look back on his actions, it might not have been the best idea to get drunk in these woods. Just the simple matter of falling and being in a difficult location for help to arrive was reason enough.

Lucas walked around in a circle, waving his arms slowly up and down, repeating Celeste. He parroted the words he could remember longer than three seconds anyway. "I call upon thee! So mote it be!"

Other than shooting him a snarky glare a couple times, she

didn't say a word to him, didn't ask him to stop. He wrongly believed it was because she found the humor in it. The encouragement made him act up more, and he began his own spell.

"Oh, blessed spirits of the woods! I call upon thee! Make my woman put out good!" He laughed and fell to his knees. "If it harm none, so mote it be!"

Lucas cracked himself up. He lay on the ground for a long time grinning like a fool. There'd be an occasional chuckle whenever he thought about the look on her face. She'd laughed too.

'Hadn't she?' Lucas was almost certain Celeste got a kick out of it, but she was so quiet now. He wasn't sure.

"Hey, babe," he said. Nothing. "Babe?" He called out louder. He tried to lift himself off the ground, but the trees started spinning, and he felt sick to his stomach. He half rolled on his side and saw her sitting twenty feet away. Her arms were wrapped around her legs, and her head rested on her knees. *'No, she is definitely not amused.'*

He got on all fours and crawled to the nearest tree, using it to pull himself upright. Several small shoots coming off the sides tore off in his hands when he used them for support. "I've got to take a leak," he announced before taking a few steps behind some trees.

Celeste hadn't seen the damage he did to the tree, but she worried nonetheless. There was still a long walk back to the car, and Lucas had drunk enough to cause a problem. The part that bothered her the most was how little she felt about it. There was no sadness, no guilt. The thoughts were going through her mind like fact.

'Lucas was going to do something dumb, and he'd pay the ultimate price. There was nothing she could do to save him.'

As it was, she could hear him laughing and carrying on. He was singing a made up song about going to the bathroom in the woods. It would've been humorous if they were anywhere else but here. He was obviously a big fan of his own lyrics by the sound of his cackling.

The most weighing on her mind was having to deal with his parents when they demanded she explain why she drug him out here knowing the risks involved. *'Like I had to drag him? He wanted to make sure I wasn't up to no good, and look at the situation he's causing.'*

There was a strange noise in front of her and off to the left. It came from the area where Lucas had wandered off. She sat upright, waiting for him to emerge, but he didn't. Then she heard something else, like a scuffling followed by gurgling noises.

Her shoulders sunk, and she hung her head. He was dead. She didn't know what happened after he left her sight, but he wasn't coming back.

Celeste continued to wait a few more minutes. Maybe she was wrong. Being alone in the woods like this could play tricks on the mind. She might've been hearing what her thoughts expected to happen. It could've been something else entirely.

Five minutes slowly ticked by while she stared at her watch. There wasn't another sound from the woods. The singing had stopped when she heard the first noise, and it hadn't started up again. Lucas was still gone too. He snored loudly when he drank, so she'd hear him if he had passed out.

She got to her feet and began to pack up her bags carefully, slowly. Everything fit, but it was pieced together like a puzzle. It was partly due to spacing, but mostly to avoid breaking anything.

Once everything was ready, she glanced at her watch again. Another twenty minutes was gone without a sign Lucas was alright. Part of her didn't want to look for him. If the tales were true, and she believed they were, she might not find any trace of him.

'What if I do? What if seeing him frightens me, and I run? What if I fall? What was it Hank said? It only takes one misstep, or something like that.'

She had to go after him. It was the right thing to do. Besides, she should've gone back to the car as soon as she figured out he was drinking. It was her own selfishness that pushed them on to her spot in the woods. She was here to do what she needed to do. It was Lucas who decided to tag along. There was no way he'd have gone back without her if she had suggested it.

The bags were at her feet. It was so tempting to pick them up and leave. Save her own skin. Something was pulling her to the area where Lucas had gone.

With a deep breath, she walked away from the bags. She'd only be a minute. This wasn't a search and rescue, putting her neck out to see if she could find him. She'd give the area a quick once over and be gone. If she was wrong, if he had simply gotten lost, that was on him.

Celeste was only a couple feet from where he left. She was standing right where he was when he was rolling around on the ground like an idiot. There was the sound of footsteps trotting through the leaves, and she stopped.

The person who stepped into the small clearing wasn't Luke. It was a woman. She had long raven hair and wore an old fashioned plain gray dress. Her beauty was unmatched by anyone Celeste had ever seen, not even in the fashion magazines her mom obsessed over. This was the lady of the woods.

Her eyes darted around looking for the quickest way to escape. Her bags could wait. Her bags could stay there in the woods forever. She brought Lucas here. He was her responsibility. The lady was going to hold her accountable for his actions.

"Celeste," the lady said with a warm smile. "I thought it time we meet." The lady wrapped her arm around Celeste's shoulders.

It was comforting. Every ounce of panic evaporated with one touch. Celeste couldn't explain how, never could in all her years, but somehow she was no longer afraid. The lady wasn't going to harm her. The lady had something else in mind.

Chapter Eleven

Life of the Party

This was too good to be true, and it fell directly into Kate's lap. Labor Day weekend was going to be extraordinary. Her friends were going to have the most frightening night of their life, and she wouldn't have to do much aside from planting a few seeds of fear. When they came back to campus on Tuesday, they'd be legends.

'And we won't have done anything more than spent a couple nights in the woods!'

Her plan was so exciting it was hard to keep it contained. This must be why people confess decades after the crime. They want people to know how smart they were. They want that credit and the accolades for out maneuvering the police. Kate wanted everyone to praise her brilliant plan, but if anyone found out, it wouldn't work.

Kate grew up near Barre, and her family spent most of the warm winter months camping. The closest she'd ever come to Ravenwood was Moss Farms. Her family used to go there when she was a kid until it closed. Her dad always took the long way around to go through Appleton instead of driving down Route 116. She knew Dunberry Road fairly well. Whenever they passed the tee intersection which led to Ravenwood, Kate would stare in the direction of the castle, hoping to see the lady in the trees. She imagined it was the same as how people in the northwest might keep an eye out for Bigfoot while on the road. There's nothing to see, but they have to look anyway.

This is how she knew they could spend the weekend at Ravenwood without ever stepping foot on the property. People believed what they wanted to anyway. This would be no different.

Lily and Rachel were from Boston. They knew the local lore surrounding Ravenwood but had never been in that part of the state. They were a different breed. To them, camping was spending the night in a Super 8. The three of them met in English 101 their first semester at Bunker Hill Community College. They hit it off immediately.

Kate counted on the two of them to write the script for her, so to speak. Once they were in the woods, those two would make it easy. Every noise would scare them. Every noise would give Kate an opportunity to convince them Ravenwood was closing in, and they had to be careful if they were to survive.

The three of them and their friend Chelsea left Boston after their last class Friday morning and headed to Barre. They had to stop at Kate's dad's house for equipment. He would be at work when they arrived, and she hadn't told him she was coming. There was a sinking feeling in the pit of her stomach when she pulled into the driveway.

Her parents announced their split spring break of her high school freshman year. She stayed with her dad mainly because all she'd ever known was in Barre including the only friends she'd ever had up to that point. That's why she's in college in Boston. She lives with her mom to attend, giving her mom some time back of what she lost. It made her feel like a traitor whenever she came back here.

The four of them loaded up her mom's car with everything they might need plus some they probably wouldn't just in case. Tents, sleeping bags, air mattresses, lanterns and the list goes on. The last thing Kate did when she went back to grab a couple cheap Styrofoam coolers since they could stack to save space in the car was leave a note for her dad on the kitchen counter. She lied, saying it was an impromptu camping trip, and he could meet everybody when they came back through on Sunday.

They weren't heading home until Monday, and her father's strong work ethic had been part of the problem during her parents' marriage. While everyone else was firing up the grill or enjoying the unofficial last weekend of summer at the lake, he'd be the only one in the office working harder than any man needed.

Soon they were on their way again. They'd stop for drinks, sandwiches and ice before hitting Route 116. The closer they got, Kate could hear it in their voices, Lily and Rachel's anyway. Their tone became higher pitched, and they started speaking much faster than usual. They were already scared. Chelsea didn't say much for most of the drive, claiming she was just tired. This made it difficult for Kate to get a read on her. It made her think Chelsea didn't believe the hype, and that could be a problem if it was true.

Kate turned onto Route 116 from Dunberry road. This way the girls might catch a glimpse of the castle as they passed. The weather was still very warm, and the trees were clinging tight to their leaves. If the view was bad, she'd drive down the lane for a better look. In fact, she might do it anyway.

The other reason for taking the direct route was to increase the odds of her plan working. Ravenwood's property ended a couple miles passed the castle. For the rest of the way to Appleton, it was owned by the Moss family, or it used to. Regardless of who owned it now, it sat empty and unkempt, probably because it was harder to get people out that close the more the legends grew around the neighboring land.

There shouldn't be a sign for Moss Farms, if any of them still existed, before she stopped right near where the two pieces of land met. The girls would all think they were at Ravenwood being so close to the property. None of them would have the slightest clue.

Kate had searched the area with satellite maps until she found the perfect spot. They'd be less than fifty yards from danger, but she didn't expect any of them to roam too far. If they did explore, she'd make sure they went in any direction but toward Ravenwood.

"Are you sure it's safe to park here?" Lily asked when Kate pulled to a stop on the shoulder of the road.

Rachel looked nervously out the car windows in every direction. "Yeah. What if it gets towed?"

"Nothing to worry about," Kate said, opening her door. "No one comes this way. If this happens to be the one in a million times when someone does, no one will follow up on a call until there's a missing person."

Chelsea didn't come into the picture until January. She had a Numerical Reasoning math class with Rachel. That's how she folded into the group. Chelsea was originally from California, but had moved to Boston her junior year of high school. Camping wasn't in her wheelhouse, but spending time in nature and hiking were.

While the other three were great, she didn't quite fit in the way she'd like, the way she was used to being a part of a group. She had always been the prankster, the life of the party. It was pretty clear that role was filled by Kate. It was cool. Boston was big enough for the both of them, but Kate was unwilling to have a partner in crime. Instead of joining together and tag teaming the other two, she needed all the accolades, all the credit, and wouldn't share a spotlight for anything.

That was all about to come to an end. Chelsea was from the opposite side of the country which might seem like a different planet to these three, but she wasn't ignorant and could figure things out easily on her own. And, yes, sometimes there was luck involved.

Kate had mentioned Moss Farms once shortly after they met. It was a miserable day in February when an ice storm kept them inside, and they were discussing summer. The conversation swerved to autumn, and Kate said she missed the caramel apples from Moss Farms she had as a child. That was it. That was enough.

A quick internet search showed her it had been a popular end of fall apple picking destination, but had been closed for over a decade. When these three began filling her head with tales of a mysterious woman who might be a ghost living in a patch of woods with a murderous appetite, Chelsea hit the keyboard again. It was easy to discover Moss Farms had been right next door.

When the plans for this weekend began to unfold, she wanted to scream at the other two. "Kate's not taking us to Ravenwood! She's planning an elaborate prank to scare the wits out of us!"

Chelsea kept it to herself, but it was hard to join in the conversations about it. The longer they talked about this camping trip the more bitter she grew. It wasn't that she didn't like Kate, but she wanted her rightful place as leader of the pack. This was, at best, a half-hearted attempt at pulling a fast one. Even if she hadn't mentioned the childhood memory, Kate really couldn't expect people not to research something on their own.

The tales of Ravenwood were nonsense. Chelsea pretended to be awed by their ghost stories in order to fit in, but it was silly. The property was off limits because it held natural dangers like ravines and wild animals. People have a tendency to want to do what they're not allowed. Ravenwood was no exception. People kept sneaking on the land, and most of them found out the hard way why they shouldn't be there. She was willing to bet most people didn't believe in any of it. The colorful stories were just more fun to tell, and they didn't go there because they followed the rules, not because they thought the trees would eat them.

It took two trips to lug everything to the spot Kate had picked out. They could've made it in one trip, but two of the girls in the group couldn't carry much at once. They worked together carrying one tent each time while Kate and Chelsea packed everything else on their backs and in their arms.

The tents were pitched and readied with air mattresses and sleeping bags. Chairs were set up and a makeshift fire pit dug out and outlined with what rocks they could find. Meanwhile, Lily and Rachel were hard at work putting the drinks and sandwiches on ice. *'This is hardly camping. Not even Kate knows what roughing it actually means.'*

After several failed attempts to start a fire, Chelsea stepped up and saved Kate from herself. *'Not even a thanks.'* Her irritation was growing. Every time she was slighted like that, it made her step up her plans to get back at Kate.

"Alright, one last thing," Kate announced, digging through a backpack. She pulled out an obnoxiously large spool of red ribbon about six inches wide. "I'm going to mark our way back to the car just in case."

"In case of what?" Lily asked.

Kate shrugged. "You know, just for safety."

It made Chelsea spin on her heels and cover her mouth. The laugh had already partially escaped, so she covered it with a cough.

"Doing alright?"

"Yeah," she told Rachel. "Water went down wrong. That's all."

With her back to them, she untwisted the cap on the bottle of water she was holding and dumped a few spoonful's on the ground. The lie wouldn't be believable if her water was still unopened.

'Why do we need a path to the car?' she thought, taking a seat near the other girls by the fire. *'From here, the car is a fairly straight shot and easy to find. We'd need the help if we explored farther off into the woods. The ribbon would help us find our way back. These two are so gullible.'*

"How's everyone doing?" Kate asked when she returned. She tossed the empty cardboard spool from the ribbon into the fire. "Comfortable? We're lucky the weather is perfect this weekend."

Lily and Rachel looked behind them for the twelfth time

since sitting down. "Fine," they said in unison.

"We'll have to take the ribbon with us when we leave and dispose of it wherever we stop for gas. Can't leave anything behind if we don't want to make the trees mad."

Chelsea chewed the inside of her lip. It was going to be hard to recruit them later, but she figured she could manage it. She didn't want to say anything until the moment she was ready to spring into action because she didn't trust them not to slip up and say something to Kate on accident. She stared into the flames half listening to another Ravenwood tall tale. Tonight was going to be epic.

The first night was simply to break them in to camping and get them used to their surroundings. There were enough noises coming from all directions to keep them on edge. By tomorrow, they'd relax a little. It meant it'd be harder for Kate, but Lily and Rachel were easy targets to scare. Chelsea was a different matter altogether. Whenever she felt like they were making progress on getting to know each other, Chelsea would clam up and shut Kate out all over again. They met seven months ago, and she still barely knew anything about her. Rachel thought Chelsea was great, and that was good enough for her. If she couldn't scare her this weekend, maybe she could convince her to help frighten the other two.

Saturday night was when she was really planning to lay down the groundwork. There was a lot more in her bag then the others realized. She was going to set up a silhouette of the lady of the woods not far from their campsite. There was also an old voice recorder of her mom's, and she filled the tape with spooky sounds to play from the trees.

Late Sunday night, she would come in for the final act.

She planned on staying awake and terrorizing the campsite in costume in the middle of the night. The thought of the girls waking up screaming made her want to laugh already, but she had to act normal. Everything was a part of the act until then.

Lily and Rachel were about to crawl out of their skin. Their chairs were right next to each other. Each noise they heard made them jump until they leaned into each other and held hands all night for comfort. When one had to venture off to find a place to use as a restroom, they both went. Part of Kate wanted to offer them a tent to share, but she thought it best for Rachel and Chelsea to stay together at least for the first night. Tomorrow, she'd try to size Chelsea up better to see if she would want to help her out.

It was dark, but it wasn't that late. Not even nine yet. It had been a long day between her science class, the drive, the loading and unloading of supplies. Still, Kate couldn't believe how tired she was.

Chelsea, on the other hand, sat quietly staring into the fire. From time to time, she'd sneak a glance at Kate and watch her eyelids droop heavy from exhaustion and her yawning increase. There's a reason she fought for root beer as the soda they brought. In her experience, it was more difficult to taste the pills in it. Plus, this brand didn't have caffeine, so it wouldn't counter the effect of the anxiety medicine she crushed up back in Boston and added to Kate's can when she stepped away for a minute.

"Well, guys, I'm beat," Kate announced. "I'm headed to bed, Lily," she said. "See you all in the morning."

As if on cue, the other two began to talk about laying down. "I wouldn't if you aren't tired," she told them.

"Otherwise, you'll be up in the middle of the night. By yourself."

That kept them glued to their chairs. Chelsea moved hers around to where they sat which was out of hearing distance of Kate's tent although she'd be knocked out soon enough.

Chelsea whispered her idea to them. Neither of them wanted any part of it. She needed them to help her move Kate across the property line. "Think of it this way. She's either going to wake up in the middle of the night terrorized or tomorrow morning mad as get out. Either way, she's going to want to leave, and we won't have to spend another night out here."

The one tidbit she left out was being honest about where they actually were. If they found out, they weren't actually at Ravenwood, there was nothing that would convince them to cross the property line. *'Besides, this way, there'll be an element of truth when we tell people where we went.'*

"Like Kate says, we just have to make sure we don't disturb anything."

A couple hours after Kate went to sleep, the three girls carried her out of her tent, still snug inside her army green sleeping bag. It was harder work than any of them expected. Lily and Rachel quietly complained the whole time, wanting to put her down as close as three feet to the tent.

"No," Chelsea told them. "She has to be far enough to not know where she is, but close enough we can hear her yelling."

'She has to be in Ravenwood.'

When Kate woke up the next morning, her head was still muddied from the pills Chelsea slipped her. As details began coming to her about where she was and what she was doing, she realized the joke was on her. The open sky littered with branches above her and the sun shining through meant the girls did something to her tent. She closed her eyes again and listened, wondering if any of them were awake yet. It wasn't a bad stunt, and she felt a little bit of pride thinking she was rubbing off on them.

She couldn't hear anything. Opening her eyes, she rolled to one side, but saw only trees. Then she sat up and looked the other way. Still only trees. That's when the panic began. She jumped to her feet and circled around until she was dizzy. There were trees everywhere.

'Oh, no,' she thought, digging through her sleeping bag for her phone. She uttered a prayer when she found it. The signal was weak, but she was able to open her map app. Just like she feared, the girls had moved her in the wrong direction.

Kate grabbed her sleeping bag, holding it haphazardly in her arms, trying to bunch it under her chin so she could see her phone screen. She'd have to be careful on her way back to the pin she had dropped at the campsite. It was about a five minute walk, but it was going to be the longest five minutes of her life. She was sweating profusely and could feel her entire body shake when she took the first step.

'I didn't hear anything,' she told herself. *'They would've been quiet bringing me out, but if something had happened, they'd have screamed. They must've made it back to camp. I can too.'*

About five feet from where she woke, she looked up and fell to her knees. Her mouth opened, but no sound came out. Directly in front of her, hanging from the lowest branch, were three pairs of shoes. They were shoes she recognized as belonging to her friends. Shoes she realized would be all that's left of them.

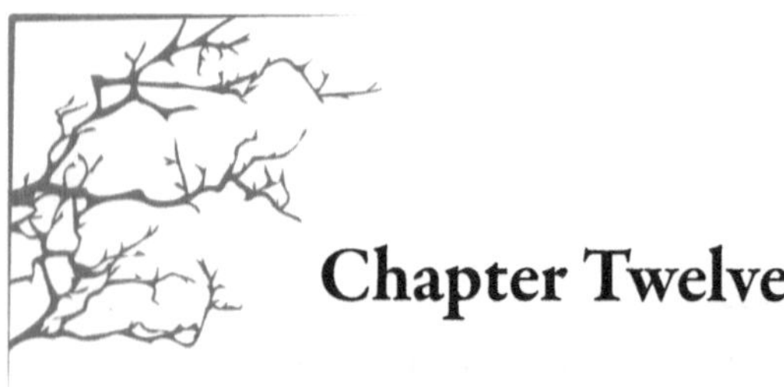

Chapter Twelve

The Other Daughter

The worries a parent suffers for their child have no end. They always thought Nikolett was a happy baby, not because of her smile or laugh, or how often her eyes lit up. It was because of how little she fussed.

Times had changed a lot since Nikolett was born. Things that are common knowledge today were not necessarily even a theory to pursue back then. No one really understood how what happened during pregnancy could affect the child.

Nikolett felt every stress her mother suffered while growing inside her. There was the strain of the end of the war, leaving her family behind and moving to a faraway land where she was not accepted by anyone, including the people most important to her husband. They had fake smiles on their faces and used sing song voices to her face, but she wasn't ignorant to the truth. Then they were turned out to the woods by those same people where she had to fight for their lives.

A decade had passed before they were granted their independence. It was a life which barely resembled freedom, but they were alive nonetheless. They spent the better part of the next winter at the mercy of the trees once more, taking shelter in a clearing while the inn was reconstructed.

If it could've been proven, the Guiness Record for longest

pregnancy would never be broken after Rozalia set it. The time flashed by for those inside the circle, so they never considered how it might have affected Nikolett until many years later. The baby was born over ten years after she was conceived. It couldn't have been good for the baby.

After every other option had been exhausted, something brought their attention back to the lengthy pregnancy. They wondered if it might be part of the cause of Nikolett's problems. She was rather unsociable. She wasn't backward by any means. The girl was capable of learning and did well in her studies. It was all of her interactions which didn't require her nose in a book where she stumbled the most.

She asked questions she ought not ask and had been raised better than to do so. She didn't understand the concepts of respect, formality, politeness and graciousness when it came to interacting with the general public. Whenever a misstep was pointed out to her, she couldn't grasp why it mattered.

In other words, she embarrassed her parents every time she was around the guests. They tucked her safely away in the family wing as often as they could, hoping to keep her away from the travelers coming and going. It was a full time job of its own. Nikolett wanted to be around the people. She enjoyed their company immensely. If only she could learn how to interact with them, she'd be a blessing for the inn. They'd have a one person welcoming committee who'd win them over to return again and again.

'I picked the wrong baby.' The thought haunted Joseph. It was both true and made him feel like the worst father who ever lived.

He chose the first born daughter without putting any real

thought into it. There were associations people made based on birth order. First borns were supposed to be more intelligent and reliable. The middle children were usually troubled and overlooked while the baby of the family was selfish and needed a little extra help simply because they weren't used to doing anything on their own.

Parents lavished the first born, helping their oldest son buy a car when he turned sixteen or celebrating their oldest daughter's accomplishments. Their oldest child could do no wrong and was the standard set for the rest of their children. Some of that enthusiasm had worn down by the time it was their second child's turn. When the youngest approached high school, there was simply no energy left. What one person views as being spoiled, having more than another, getting whatever they desired, being able to do what they want when they want, was a parent's way of checking out because their job had grown tiresome.

Everywhere you looked birth order mattered. The deals made in dark fairy tales always required payment of a first born child. Reports of a new baby born into royalty was met with headlines heavily discounting the subsequent children. It was the queen's duty to produce an heir and, hopefully, a spare. The first born received all the glory while the backup stayed in the background. It's all over society, planting seeds in the mind about the oldest child. All of these things regarding the first born he had read or heard about throughout his life, and it helped shape that decision, allowing him to make it without giving it proper consideration.

Joseph didn't see how any of this applied to him and Rozalia or their baby. This wasn't a fairy tale, and they certainly weren't royalty. Birth order shouldn't make a big difference because the oldest usually referred to a child who had his parents to himself for three years before the next sibling came along. In this case, Nikolett was merely the child sitting closest to the exit.

As much as he loved Nikolett, he sometimes wondered how the other child was faring. His daughter had a lot of difficulties which would eventually be attributed to the elongated pregnancy. She needed a lot of special attention. Given their home life and work were combined, it wasn't so bad. Their daughter could be there in the inn, running around and playing while they worked, except she didn't run amok. She didn't leave her parents' side, never liked to be alone, and barely spoke, but when she did, it was never without complication. She was sharp as a tack when it came to her studies, but that intellect wasn't reflected in anything else.

There were health problems as well. The doctors were always surprised. These conditions usually weren't seen in patients until they were much older in age. For a long time, they believed their lineage would end with them. Someone like Nikolett would never find a suitable husband with all of her hardships.

Joseph always felt like the poor health was punishment from Ravenwood for giving the other child up for adoption. He wished the trees would punish him instead of his daughter. She had no say in his decisions when she was born. It was a torment he suffered alone because he couldn't confide in Rozalia.

Every week there was a meeting with a doctor. Every month brought along a new concern which needed to be checked out. The poor girl was allergic to almost everything not found naturally at Ravenwood. The meals she ate had to be specially prepared. For a while, her parents ate what she did to offer support, but the diet was bland and left much to be desired. They began nibbling at meal time with their daughter before having their real supper later in secret.

Nikolett was on more daily medications than most people past their prime. Her rheumatoid arthritis was always flaring up. New eyeglasses barely lasted a year before a stronger lens was needed to help her see. She was the youngest old person any of the staff had ever met.

There was no one else who could handle it like she did. Maybe it was because she had never known anything different. Maybe it was because she felt blessed to not have to face the evil lurking in the woods like her mother did every morning.

To his surprise, suitors did come around. It had to be Rozalia's arranging because putting his daughter on the market was not something he was keen about doing. They came from across the state with a couple stragglers from Connecticut, and one traveled from as far as New York City. It made Joseph beam with pride to see his daughter attract such handsome young men who'd make fine providers for their families even if he wasn't ready to let her go just yet.

Then he learned it wasn't Nikolett they were interested in at all. It was Ravenwood. Every one of them were only trudging through the cover of wooing his daughter because they believed the inn would one day be hers which made it theirs.

Selling the inn wasn't an option for Joseph and Rozalia. They had never considered the possibility of their daughter selling it. The trees wouldn't react kindly. If there was any hope of escaping the clutches of the woods, the sale would have to wait until he and Rozalia were gone. By the looks of her, she had two lifetimes left to live. They both retained youthful appearances, but Rozalia barely aged a day. Her body hadn't caught up to the present day aches, pains, and overall general roughness of Joseph's either. It was like she was suspended in time. Nikolett seemed older than her mother, and they had already discussed their concerns they might outlive their daughter.

A young man who forced the sale after the inn was transferred could meet an unfortunate fate, but he could also drag their daughter to the depths of the fires with him. Poor Rozalia watched the men interact with Nikolett seeing nothing of the truth. There were comical balloon hearts beating wildly in place of her eyes, and everything she said dripped with the tune of a love song from long ago. She had always been in love with the idea of love, a hopeless romantic at heart.

Once her blinders were removed, the men who came to Ravenwood in the hopes of landing a vast piece of land with a castle shaped revenue system in place were sent packing before they made it to the desk to register a room. It dampened Nikolett's spirits to see her suitors stop, but her father reassured her she was too young for marriage yet. There'd be many more when the time was right.

'But would there be?' He wasn't as confident as his words made him sound.

Months later he walked down the grand hall to the sound of his daughter's laughter. It was music to his ears. Her moments of joy were rare. The deep masculine voice which followed was foreign to him, but it was too obvious this man was capturing his daughter's attention. Joseph took off at a run to put an end to it, but when he rounded the corner, the first person he saw was his wife.

His temper waged war on his body. He wouldn't say anything in front of the staff, but later, in their room, he'd remind her why they put an end to this foolishness.

It was, in a way, worse than he thought. The man his daughter was batting her lashes at was not the same stock as her previous visitors. This man was a little older, late twenties, and already his hairline was receding. The suit he wore hung off his body, likely his father's, and had been patched numerous times. His hands were rough showcasing a life made from working hard. It was a respectable pursuit, but one which didn't guarantee a future for Nikolett.

This man was poor, and he was uneducated as Joseph would soon learn. There was nothing in his background or family tree which would lend to a successful union. He was also not what Joseph had in mind for his daughter's husband.

Nikolett didn't care about such things. Her opinion of the man was formed by the way he made her smile. He didn't mind helping her when her joints ached. The thick glasses she wore didn't detract from the beauty he saw in her. His rough hands told her this man could protect her. He had the strength and the know-how. Of all her suitors, Nikolett believed the best had been saved for last.

Joseph worried the man was only out for money, hoping there was something to obtain here. He tried to warn him away, saying the inn was a money pit requiring constant attention. That wasn't far removed from the truth. He also said it couldn't be sold. The only real income from it was a place to live.

This young man eagerly accepted the news. With his skill and work ethic, he'd be able to help with the repairs. It might save enough cost to cover some small updates to the building. Honestly, if Joseph wasn't unsure of the man's true intentions, he'd be a welcome addition to the family.

Seeing the two together made Joseph think. *'Did I choose the wrong baby?'* Marrying off his daughter wasn't a priority for him, but his wife dreamt about a large event. It would be the biggest wedding in the state or nothing. All of the fuss seemed a waste on Nikolett who likely wouldn't be able to manage the walk down the aisle. He wondered about the other daughter, the one he left behind.

The idea had bounced around in his mind for a long time, but he finally decided to track down the family who adopted Nikolett's sister. They weren't hard to find. It wasn't as difficult as it would've been had he not heard the father's name spoken numerous times at the hospital. There was even a conversation about all the people meeting them at home in Dunberry to welcome the new addition to their family.

Edward Sullivan still lived on Maple Street in the quiet country town. He and his wife never had another child, and Joseph wondered if they had tried. Many nights he'd take the long route home and cruise around their block a couple times. He'd tell Rozalia the lines were long, or he got swept up in a conversation with a stranger at a gas station to explain his delay. All he wanted was a glimpse, a quick peek through a window to see how different the two were if he could tell anything from a glance, but he was never able to observe anything.

On one occasion when everything had gone smoothly in Appleton, freeing his time to be home much earlier than expected, he made his way to Dunberry. Dusk was settling in, and the lights in all the homes were being flicked on as he drove down the street where the Sullivan's lived. He parked two blocks down and walked back, leaning against the tree growing along the property border near the sidewalk. He wouldn't hang out long enough to draw suspicion from the neighbors, just long enough to see for himself.

Fifteen minutes passed, and he was about to leave. He'd watch the couple move into the kitchen, but their daughter wasn't to be seen.

"What do you think you're doing?"

The voice bellowing from behind made him jump. He spun around to see a man he barely recognized as the older version of the father crying softly in the hospital hallway sixteen years earlier. Edward Sullivan had gone out his back door and snuck up on Joseph.

"I'm so sorry," Joseph cleared his throat.

The man sneered. "I didn't ask if you were sorry. What do you want?" he barked.

"I just..." Joseph looked up at the house. "I was..." There was no easy way to explain why he'd been lurking around.

"Coming to take Margaret back, are you?" Sullivan squared his shoulders. "You'll have to go through me."

"What?" Joseph took a step back, but the man came forward, not letting Joseph put any distance between them. "No, I'm just..."

'Take Margaret back.' He recognized Joseph all these years later.

"We were elated when we took Margaret home, but I'm not sure we would've agreed if we'd known you'd track us down years later and spy on us."

"That's not... I'm not..." Joseph stuttered. Edward Sullivan towered over him and was probably twice his weight. If he took a swing, Joseph didn't stand a chance.

Joseph sighed heavily. "I was just curious," he said, hanging his head.

With a glance at the house, Edward said, "I can't let you in. I'm not sure how my wife would feel about it. Margaret doesn't know she's adopted either."

"No, I understand. That's why this is as close as I would ever come."

The two men stood there in the growing darkness. Neither really sure what to say.

"How's she doing?" Joseph asked. "I had been wondering if..." He cut himself off, alarmed at how easily he almost finished the sentence with, "I chose the wrong baby."

"Wondering if you made the right choice of babes that day?" The words came out of the man's mouth with such intense certainty Joseph realized this man had been having the same thoughts.

"No, uh... I mean." Joseph stammered trying to find a way to back pedal out of this mess.

"Name's Ed," the man said, extending a hand. "Ed Sullivan."

Joseph shook his hand, feeling thankful he let the subject drop.

"Let's go for a walk," Ed said, briefly grasping Joseph's shoulder before turning to leave his house behind them.

They made it a block before Ed said anything else. "Margaret's doing well in most ways. She loves music. Plays the piano."

"Any health problems?" That's the only thing on Joseph's mind. He wanted to know if the other twin affected the same way.

"Why do you ask?"

Joseph went for broke and told him the truth. "Because Nikolett has more than I can remember."

"No, she's perfectly healthy. There's nothing wrong with her of note."

He had expected it to make him feel bad, but it didn't. Actually, now that he heard Margaret was healthy, he was happy he had chosen Nikolett. The Sullivan's didn't come across as bad people, but it was hard to tell. People had done horrible things to their own blood, and it worried him what might've happened to Nikolett if she had been the one adopted.

"There is one oddity though."

"What is that?" Joseph was curious.

"Religion," Ed said, shaking his head. "Not just ours, but all religions. She studies them all. It's always been a fascinating subject for her."

It didn't seem too odd to Joseph. Many people had an interest which drained all their free time. Margaret's just happened to be learning about what others believed.

"Every day she has a new favorite religion she talks about converting to," Ed shook his head. "I wouldn't have thought much about it if it weren't for the background of where you folks are from," Ed continued.

Joseph stopped walking. His car was just ahead, and he was feeling like he should be on his way soon. "I wasn't sure if you knew."

"Let's just say you're not the first parent to have questions they hoped the other one could answer."

As he shook Ed's hand again before leaving, he was aware of two things. Ed had visited Ravenwood with similar questions and dark thoughts just as Joseph had been experiencing. This was the last time either of the two men would try to track down the other family, but they'd always be entangled somehow.

Chapter Thirteen

Without Permission

If he got caught, it would be his third strike. Since being banned from the inn, he had been caught sneaking onto the property to do an investigation twice. The first time it happened the Weavers, while highly angered, simply warned him not to come back. The second time, however, the police were involved.

The office who responded to the call pretty much told him he was the most idiotic man alive, just not in those words. "If you're familiar with the dangers of Ravenwood, why would you take the risk? Do you have a death wish? Is that what you're hoping to accomplish?"

No charges were pressed, but not because the Weavers didn't insist. It was because the police force convinced them to give Ryan one more chance. No officer wanted to do a thorough search of the woods even if a Weaver woman accompanied him. Lucinda made it crystal clear if Ryan was ever discovered on the property again, he was to be arrested.

But, she was no longer in charge. Young Lorelei was calling the shots before she was of age. She was essentially in charge as acting manager while she was in college. Her mom signed the business over to her before her graduation day.

As soon as it was official, changes were made. Little things like the doom and gloom pictures being added to the website instead of painstakingly angling shots to showcase Ravenwood in a better light. When Ryan heard the radio commercial advertising it as a "notoriously haunted" destination where you could book lodging or come for a meal and explore the walking trails, he knew it was time for him to proposition the one Weaver woman who might give him permission.

Unfortunately, the meeting with her was cryptic at best. He set up an appointment to speak to her in person thinking it might work in his favor better than a phone call.

"I'm really happy you reached out," she told him. "I'm a big fan of yours."

"And, I'm a big fan of yours as well," he chuckled.

"You're welcome back in the manor anytime you wish to visit." Inviting him to stay and even conducting research was something she offered multiple times during their conversation, but she never welcomed him to set up in the woods. "I never agreed with your banishment."

"I am so happy to hear you say that." Ryan also believed Lorelei was on his side. Others mocked him for it. They thought the impression he had of a teenager he talked to briefly in the woods wasn't enough to hold out so much hope. "So I can bring my equipment along?"

"Yes, at any time, but if you want to do a full scale investigation, it needs to be arranged in advance. We'll have to schedule it at a time when you're away from the guests. I don't want to interrupt anybody's stay here."

"I can understand that," Ryan nodded. It would be costly to book the entire inn, but worth it.

"If you come out here on a whim and want to bring a

camera or a recorder, I have no problem as long as you do it discreetly. If a guest complains, I'll have to say something about it."

"Of course," Ryan agreed. This meeting was going as good as he expected, but now for the important part. "I also wanted to talk to you about setting up my equipment in the woods."

Lorelei sighed, and said, "I would love it. I, personally, would have no problems with it. If I'm being honest, I would love to be out there watching it, but I am unable to give permission for that."

"Why?" Ryan didn't want to sound angry or like a child throwing a tantrum. "Is it insurance? I'd be happy to sign a waiver," he added.

"No, it's nothing like that."

"I've been itching to come back for so long. I've thought about just doing it anyway. I can't count how many times I started to plan a trip out to 116 and just sneaking onto the property. The only thing stopping me was the threat of being arrested," Ryan confessed. He wasn't sure why he admitted to her the extremes he was almost willing to take. The words just flew out before he could stop them.

"Well, I'm not having anybody arrested, but I can't give you permission."

"You're not going to tell me why?" he asked. It was a shot in the dark. Once he knew the reason, he could try to find a solution to his problem.

"There's a lot of things about me which are contradictory," Lorelei said. "I believe in spirits. I believe other forces are in this world we don't understand, supernatural forces. I also have faith. I don't want to give permission for anyone to explore these woods. If something happened to them, I would feel like their blood is on my hands. I don't need anyone's death marking my soul."

Ryan nodded slowly. He had long wondered how the Weavers lived with themselves. Ravenwood was a giant trap for the woods to obtain unwitting human sacrifices. It was their rules which made them shake off the responsibility of all the bloodshed. "And I don't suppose there's anything I could do to convince you?"

"I can't give anybody permission to come into the woods, but I can tell you I'm not having anybody arrested if they do. If someone wanders on the property and makes it out alive, whatever they experienced while they were out there is punishment enough."

It would've made Ryan laugh if there wasn't something eerily ominous about it. "Well, thank you for your time," he said, standing from his chair. "I will definitely stop at reception to book a visit for me and my wife. I want to do a full scale investigation as soon as possible. If you could check your calendar and let me know, I will move around everything to make it work."

"I'll let you know by the end of the week," Lorelei promised. She walked him out of the office door, and told him, "Again, I'm sorry. I can't give you permission, but I won't arrest you either."

'Wait a minute.' Something clicked when she repeated it this time. *'In her own way, she's telling me I can do it.'*

It was nearing four in the morning on the second night of their investigation at Ravenwood. The activity was finally starting to settle down. Everything was relative. Calming for

Ravenwood carried exponentially more activity than most other haunts he'd investigated.

The inn had been divided into two sections for this weekend. They thoroughly explored the upper floors with the guest rooms on the first night and saved the best for last. Cameras, EMF readers, REM Pods, everything in their arsenal were still set up throughout the entire inn regardless of the area they were focusing on in case something was picked up.

Four of the six people on his crew came with him. The other two weren't coming to Ravenwood even with the promise of never having to leave the castle. It worked out fine. Once his former colleagues and other experts in the field learned what he was up to, he welcomed five guest investigators to join this haunted expedition. He wound up with a larger crew than usual. Even so, the nine of them were run ragged both nights.

It cost an arm and a leg to book the castle for the entire weekend. Lorelei refused to allow Chasing Ghosts to stir up any spirit's wrath while anyone else was staying at the inn. Good thing the network paid for it. There was so much footage, so much activity captured. This was more than every investigation he had ever done, whether it was his or he was collaborating with someone else. All of those findings together didn't equal two nights at Ravenwood. The network was already considering making it into a special instead of having the castle being part of his regular season run. It had even been discussed to do a three part, hour long each, documentary mini-series on it.

Ryan wasn't against the idea, but he wanted to take it a step further. He'd like to see an entire season devoted to

Ravenwood. Interviews with the locals, past guests who stayed there, the lore, eye witness accounts peppered in alongside the activity which could possibly be linked to the people who went missing from the area. He'd wait until he had footage from the woods to pitch the idea. The trees alone would provide enough material for the twelve episodes his seasons lasted.

That was tomorrow night. Right now, he had to concentrate on finishing the castle. His crew had spent the better part of the last hour packing away the upstairs. They had moved down to the first floor where the sensors in the office were relentless.

Most of it centered near the desk. The handset of the phone would flip off the hook. Drawers would open. Framed pictures would be tilted on the wall. One angle of footage showed a picture spinning around before it dropped to the floor.

After the first night, Lorelei wasn't surprised to hear her office, especially the desk, was a hot spot. She felt the spirits every day. It had slowly started becoming that way since the beginning, but the activity increased dramatically before she was born. Her grandmother was the first one who had to empty the desk. It's there for function only, not utility. It's great for having a flat surface to write on, but that's about it. Nothing can be stored in it. Nothing you want to keep in good condition to use again anyway. Lorelei has several large planners kept in a tote with important documents, forms, and supplies to do her job, and the tote got drugged along with her when she works every day.

The office bathroom was another loaded hot spot of the inn. The spirit who called that room home could be felt without any of his expensive high tech ghostly surveillance gadgets. It usually implied a violent death, either by the nature the individual died or the emotion surrounding it, leading up to the end. Both were highly plausible for this place.

All of the interviews with staff made it clear nothing would make them enter that room. A few went so far as to claim they would suffer the embarrassment of soiling themselves before using that particular bathroom. Lorelei acknowledged there was a fog of despair which clouded the room, but she claimed it didn't prevent her from using it when necessary. The layer of dust on the counter in the bathroom suggested not only did Lorelei always use a different bathroom, but she had also not been in there to discover housekeeping had been avoiding the room as well.

Any piece of equipment his crew put in the room offered immediate and numerous readings. The responses triggered would increase until the equipment malfunctioned. After losing a couple of very expensive ghost hunting tools because they short circuited and fried, he decided to leave the room alone. The door was left open with a camera angled inside hoping to catch something.

The most interesting detail about the office was there were no recorded deaths here. A little ways farther down in the breakroom was where a maintenance man named Jerry had lost his life in an accident. The door had swung into him hard enough to knock him into a glass encased bulletin wall which shattered. Fragments of glass stabbed through his skull. Many believed the death was no accident, and the history of Ravenwood alone was enough to support those claims.

Still nothing had ever been reported anywhere else in this

part of the inn. Two others had gone missing that night. Becky and Viv had long been presumed of running away after Jerry's death. The threat of the castle and the property drove them away. They were never seen or heard from again. It was enough for Ryan to suspect something far more treacherous happened, but he couldn't figure out why Ravenwood would hide two bodies and not the third.

Many former guests as well as employees had gone missing. Each with their own story. Some believed to have run for personal reasons while others were assumed to have met their fate in the woods after stepping off the trails. The activity in this area piqued his curiosity as to what really happened in these rooms.

Did the woods transport them out of the castle? Maybe with the lady's help? Or were they consumed by the inn itself? It would require much more than two nights to dig into this mystery.

Ryan didn't take anyone into the woods with him that night. None of the team were aware of what he had planned. The only ones who knew anything were two of the producers from the network, and that was only so he'd have someone to call for bail if Lorelei had him arrested. She had told him several times she wouldn't, but in his experience, people had a way of changing their minds when push came to shove.

It was exciting out there, setting his equipment up alone. He'd been managing a crew for so long, taking direction from the producers over which pieces to guide his focus. The woods reminded him of how it was in the beginning when he first started down this career. There were countless times when it was just him, a shoddy video camera, and a voice recorder.

The equipment had improved drastically, but the thrill was the same.

"I can't give you permission, but I won't arrest you either." Lorelei's words played on an endless loop in his brain. He had wanted to ask her about it, to get some kind of clarification, but he didn't dare risk it. If he was right about what she meant, she already knew where he was, but there was that nagging thought he might be wrong. If that was the case, he didn't want to tip her off and have her block him from going into the woods.

He had hiked for quite a while before deciding on a location. There were several spots he was interested in, like Earl, but that was too close to the Inn. For years, he had mapped out the areas where people reported any kind of activity, mostly where bodies were found, as best as he could with the information he could gather. Now that he was here, he ignored all the pinpoints on his map.

Ryan chose to let the woods lead him. He hadn't been in this field since college without learning to pick up cues. While he wasn't born a natural psychic or medium, he'd paid attention to how his body reacted in the presence of spirits. He left his van with a bag strapped to his back and a utility duffel which took two hands to carry. Once he was inside the tree line, he played a game of hot and cold with the vibes he felt.

Every few feet, he'd pause and concentrate on the energy around him. When the trail began to run cold, he'd go back to where he had been and set off somewhere new. He could play this game all night and would probably still never find the area with the most energy present, but the place he picked to stop was quite dynamic. He felt it over his entire body. His hair was on end, goosebumps bred more goosebumps. He felt out of place and sick to his stomach. This spot was ripe with a presence he was going to be certain not to anger.

This was why he was quite surprised how quickly he tired. As soon as everything was in place, he made himself comfortable for a night of watching the readings. Once the wee hours of morning came, he'd venture a short distance away and ask some questions, hoping to pick up something on his recordings.

As soon as everything was ready, he could barely keep his eyes open. There was a thermos of coffee in one of the bags which was meant to help him make it through the last hour or two when exhaustion typically came into play. It wasn't even midnight before he started sipping from it, hoping for a little boost of energy. There was one cup of it left, if that, and he could barely keep his eyes open.

'It has to be the trees,' he thought. *'This has never happened to me before.'*

Almost all of his investigations were done overnight. Third shift was what he was used to working. Not only that, but he'd just pulled two all-nighters in a row. He had slept all day today and should be able to make it to the hours just before dawn without any difficulty. Instead, he kept getting up and marching around, doing jumping jacks or anything else he could think of to get the blood pumping and wake him up.

He didn't remember dozing off in his chair. Every time it felt like his eyes might close, he stood right up and moved around. It's why waking up in his van gave him quite a start.

Ryan gripped the wheel and glanced all around him frantically. The first thing he noticed was the thermos on the passenger seat. His bags were in the back. Even without going through them, they looked fairly well packed. *'How on earth do I not remember coming back?'*

A knock on the driver's window caused him to jump and twist hard enough to pull a muscle in his side, and he screamed.

A very bemused looking Lorelei stood next to the van on the road. When he finally looked fully in her direction, she smiled and motioned for him to roll down the window.

Ryan patted his pockets then saw the key in the ignition. He turned it to accessory and pressed the button.

Before he could say anything, she asked, "Are you alright?"

"Yeah," he nodded. "Nothing hurt but my pride. Hang on."

He rolled the window back up and climbed into the back of the van, opening his bags. Everything was there. Every last piece of equipment he had hauled through the woods for at least an hour was here without any memory of moving it.

He opened the rear doors of the van and jumped out on the shoulder. Lorelei came around the corner of the van and stopped.

"I had a feeling," she said. Her eyes twinkled in the morning light. "I thought I should come check on you."

Ryan shook his head. There were a number of emotions going through him, but right now, embarrassment over his child like shriek when she knocked was the primary one. "I don't understand what happened."

"I told you I can't give you permission to investigate out here," Lorelei said. She looked off into the woods. "It's not my permission you need."

Chapter Fourteen

Trinity Church

Mandy pulled into her driveway after working all day, and for the first time in the two months since her move, she felt like she was coming home. The contents of her California house had been successfully moved across country, and the new furniture she had picked out for the dining room as well as a few other odd pieces she had purchased for around the house had been delivered. Everything was unpacked and put away.

A regular routine had been established between her work schedule and personal life. She had found new doctors, a new favorite grocery store and gym. She was settling into her new house, new job and new life. Today was not only payday, but she had plans this weekend. When she turned onto her street, she had excitement about what the next few days held, not anxiety over if she had made the right decision in moving. As pleasing as the feeling was, it wasn't something she could get used to experiencing. She had to stay on alert. If she let her guard down, they'd find her.

Mandy chose to live in Barre for two reasons. It was a short commute to her new job. Most importantly, she chose it because it was near the center of the state. Many in her family had moved to the coast near the Boston area, but several still lived in the western part of the state where her great-grandma had been born.

It wasn't that her family was bad necessarily. In many ways, they were good people. They supported each other, loved each other, and were extremely kind. She'd pretend to fly in a couple times a year for holidays or during the summer to visit. One of them would pick her up from the airport under the assumption she had just arrived from California. It was wrong to deceive them, but she couldn't allow herself to be sucked back in to that way of life if they'd have her. Some days she didn't know which would be worse: given up her new found identity or being shunned by the only people she had in her life.

She'd talk to them over the phone or by email and comment on their social media posts. Their relationship would be much the same as it had been with the exception of never disclosing how close she currently lived. It was a ruse made easier to pull thanks to the changing times. When she first moved to California, her phone number had to change. That's not the case anymore. Landlines were non-existent, and she could keep the same cellular number wherever she lived.

Her family never visited her after she moved out of state. She offered all of them a place to stay if they ever took a vacation out on the west coast. In the years she lived in Lemon Grove, there was only one time any of them had made it that far. Her Uncle Marty brought his family out to visit LA and go to Disneyland. Mandy didn't know they had been so close to her until after they returned home and shared vacation photos online.

She asked him why they didn't visit while they were there. His response was she lived two hours from the theme park. It was too far to drive for the daily excursions they had planned.

"I could've come up and spent a day with you. I would have if I had known you were so close," she explained.

"It was my family's vacation though," Uncle Marty replied. The words stabbed her in the chest. "You can take in the sights whenever you like. Besides, we'll see you at Thanksgiving."

'Thanksgiving is still four months away,' she thought. His words were a little rude, but not at all shocking. It's how they were.

Her family wasn't without love and affection. It was just wrapped up in a religion which bordered on being a cult, and it was disguised as holding each other accountable in a manner the good Lord above dictated.

Their religious background was a blessing and a curse. Her entire childhood all the way through college was a scourge. Dating wasn't even to be mentioned by her, let alone allowed. Mandy grew up in a home without a television. Their entertainment was taking care of the home and worship. The books she read had to be approved by her mother who even went so far as to excuse her from a ninth grade English unit because the book "To Kill a Mockingbird" went against their religion. After that, Mandy arrived at school early every day and stayed late whenever she could to avoid bringing her homework home ever again.

Her Great Uncle Simon had a job at a company that moved to Boston. The rest of the family looked down on him for moving his wife and children there. He didn't want to give up the pension believing he was too old to start over again in a new position. Eventually, the family got over it, but it was the farthest any of them had moved until Mandy went out west.

The only reason no one objected to it was because of what

happened to her at Ravenwood. She had survived while her friends did not. Her family should have been joyous, overcome with relief she had been discovered with minimal injuries. They possibly could have had some form of a survivor's guilt since she was fine while the families of her friends grieved their loss.

Of course, that's not her family's style. One cousin flat out asked her, "What deal did you make with the devil in order to live?"

They took her surviving as a sign evil was a part of her. The premonitions she'd been having most of her life didn't help that opinion much either. She'd tried to hide them. It wasn't anything she openly discussed with them. She knew better than that. Still, there were times when it was obvious she knew something she had no explanation for knowing. They didn't argue about her moving to California because they felt more at ease with her gone.

Even though they didn't live nearby, Mandy never let her guard down. She had seen a cousin of hers driving down the streets of Barre shortly before she found a house. She could recognize her family anywhere by the stickers littering the tailgate advertising their religion and warning nonbelievers to repent. She'd also seen one of her brothers at a Rite Aid. Neither of them noticed her because they didn't know to be watching for her. The day would come when she would turn the aisle in some random store and came face to face with someone in her family. It was a waking nightmare that gnawed at her and kept her awake at night.

There was something bigger than that risk at stake. She had to be here. Soon, she'd be at Ravenwood. The lady didn't provide many details, so soon was relative. All that mattered was she held up her end of it.

Fridays were her favorite day of the week. Her four day work week allowed her an eight to ten hour stretch where she didn't have to worry as much. She still watched for them, but it was highly unlikely she'd ever run into one of them on that day.

She started the day off at the gym. It was located in a strip mall. No one in her family would ever get a membership because worrying about the way your body looked was vain. The health benefits to losing weight and staying in shape didn't matter. Nor would they visit the tattoo shop next door because marking up the body God gave you was a sin. The Chinese restaurant on the other side of the gym was another place they'd never go. Her family was particular about what businesses they supported, and the list was short.

While they wouldn't step foot inside these places, they would stand outside of them and pepper the unsuspecting public with pamphlets drawn up by her mom or one of her aunts, detailing specifically how they would spend all of eternity in the fires of hell if they didn't do something now to correct the path their life was heading down. *I can't believe I ever thought this was normal,* she sighed as she parked her car. *'That all families spend quality time forcing their religious beliefs on others.'*

'But I won't see them standing near the entrance doors today,' Mandy thought. No, it was a weekday. Weekdays meant work. The men would be earning money to support their families. Women would be taking care of the home and the little children. The older kids would be in school.

Still, she couldn't let her guard down completely. Before she left her car, she would pull her hair up under her hat and put on her oversized sunglasses which covered half her face. As she walked to the gym, she would keep her head pointed to the ground, watching each step her foot made, glancing around out of the corners of her eyes, and hoping today wasn't the day they'd discover her. *'Of course, if one of them was frequenting any of these businesses, their need for secrecy would be dire and might play into my favor.'*

She'd been safe so far and hadn't run into any of them. On the actual weekend, she didn't like to leave her house before evening regardless of how important it was, at least not on Saturday. If any of her family were out in the area, and she knew at some point in time they would be if they hadn't already been since she moved in, she wasn't going to risk running into them. They'd be out in the morning and finish up in the afternoon. They wouldn't be here at supper time. On Sunday, they did nothing but worship.

Absolutely nothing but worship. There were many Sundays she could remember as a child sitting through endless sermons, feeling as though she might starve to death. Eating was a glaring secondary importance to religion.

She had prepared a number of excuses for the inevitable day when they recognized her. The most likely candidate to date, the favorite of her lies, was to say she had been planning a surprise visit home, and she would tailor it to wherever she was and what she was doing when she was caught.

"I'm just picking up a few things, getting a gift to surprise mom."

"I had to get a prescription filled because I left mine at home."

"I knew father would be at work, so I was timing it to

surprise everyone at once."

The one thing she feared as much as she longed for it was they wouldn't care. They'd treat her with indifference. She'd been in California long enough for them to disregard her as family. It had its benefits, sure. She hardly ever saw them anymore. The one thing getting away did was open her eyes to how they really were. Years ago, she realized she was alone in the world, but she wasn't ready to make that official either. They were the only family she had after all, at least for now. The move to the woods would cut the ties with them, but until then, they were all she had.

It took her until high school to realize just how different her family was from everyone else. Growing up, she had no clue they were the ones who weren't normal. While their religion wasn't like everyone else's, she thought everyone worshiped as much as they did and held fast to their beliefs. Her friends in high school opened her eyes to how devout they were by comparison. California was where she realized the church created by her great grandma was barely distinct from a cult.

It's like making excuses for a bad relationship. It's hard to see how bad it is until the circumstances have been removed. As they say, hindsight is twenty-twenty. *'And sometimes you can't see the forest for the trees,'* she smiled.

Great Grandma Margaret was the one who began the Trinity Church. The name was longer when it started out. Trinity had been more of a nickname, and over time, it stuck. Margaret Sullivan wouldn't have stood for it. The shortening of the name of their religion would've been a sin in her mind, and she'd have forbidden it.

By the time she created the church with the help of her

grandson, she was long past her prime. She didn't live much longer than the establishing of her own religious sect. Her grandson, Jack, who was Mandy's father was so enamored by her that he changed his name to Sullivan before he married to prevent it from dying out with her.

The concept of the Trinity was three parts. They were the three things you needed to live a good life to please the Lord. The first was an obvious belief in God. The bible they used was the King James Version, and it was taught to the letter. Every day began and ended with prayer. The bible was read daily as much and for as long as possible. Members of her family had been known to hold full conversations in bible quotes with everyone present being able to comprehend every word being communicated.

Church was attended every Sunday. The first sermons were held in Margaret's own living room, but the congregation had grown enough to support a small building constructed on the edge of her property which she left to Jack. Church service would last until whoever officiated lost their voice. It could continue on until sundown on some days.

When she was a child, she was eager to greet the newcomers. There wasn't much chance to talk during the sermons, and they lasted far too long typically for anyone to want to hang around afterward. It still provided enough of a change to make the day feel less tedious. As an adult, she wondered what someone had to be going through to find comfort in the arms of a cult.

The second part was staying healthy. It included what was put into your body. They limited processed foods and sugar. There was no junk food or desserts allowed. That was only the beginning. Medications were limited and most were considered unnecessary. No one dared do drugs or drink. That was a direct sin. No tattoos or piercings, and the face was not to be obscured with makeup.

Birthdays were celebrated with fruit. If one was lucky, they might be treated with a gelatin bowl. Mandy only invited friends for one gathering back when she was in the fourth grade. The relentless teasing at school for months afterward made certain she never had a friend over again. Her celebration began with bible reading followed by her favorite meal. The dessert was honeydew, and the only gift given was a bible, a used one at that. It had been her mom's first bible which was why it was special.

The rumors at school didn't have anything to do with the religious backdrop which was part of why it took Mandy so long to put two and two together. Instead, she was berated for being poor. Her family was so destitute their birthday gifts were hand me downs.

The Trinity rounded out with nature. Live right by nature. Don't litter. Don't be wasteful. Eat what you catch. Replace what you use. Take with you what you brought. In the western part of the state, there was a long running joke about the church. Which came first? Was Ravenwood first, and the church sprung up adapting modern religion to the belief trees would seek out vengeance if they had been harmed? Or did the church come first, and the tales of Ravenwood grew out of what it preached? It had made Mandy the butt of some teasing in high school because of it. Unluckily for her, all of the kids had many other reasons to make fun of her.

After her near brush with death in those woods, things in

her family took a turn for the worse. Visiting the property at Ravenwood had never been listed as a sin until Mandy survived the woods. The third part of the Trinity was about the entire natural world, not one small section of the state. After she survived, most of the preaching was tailored to mention Ravenwood by name. Nature demanded respect, and that's what it should receive. Ravenwood wanted to be left alone, and they granted Ravenwood that peace.

Mandy hadn't done that. Because of it, three of her friends paid the ultimate price. It was made very clear to her, in no uncertain terms, the deaths of her friends would be on her soul come judgment day. It was the only reason she was allowed to leave the cult so easily. Her family was afraid they would be held accountable by association. She saw it in their eyes constantly after that day. They believed her soul couldn't be saved.

She moved to California to get away, to escape it, to put it as far behind her as possible because it was the only way she'd be able to heal. The truth was her family, their church, wanted nothing to do with that piece of land. Those woods were now a part of Mandy which meant she was on the outside too.

All of these beliefs had begun with Great Grandma Margaret. *Did she know? Did she know how our family was connected to Ravenwood?* Mandy glanced around the sidewalk of the strip mall before leaving the gym, making sure the coast was clear. *She had to have known, and it was a secret she took to her grave. If she ever shared it with anyone, it would've been her grandson Jack, but he never told a soul.* It was a secret which would've been lost to everyone in their family forever if the lady of the woods hadn't advised Mandy of her namesake and her rightful place among the trees.

Chapter Fifteen

Unlucky in Love

What finally turned Lucinda around was the same thing too many lost souls put their faith in: love. Timothy was a catch in so many ways. He had looks, education, a good upbringing, charisma for days, and was an all-around genuinely good person. He didn't see Ravenwood as a money making scheme or a burden. He also didn't quite see it for what it was. According to Timothy, the woods were simply misunderstood.

Taking her family's advice, Lucinda waited until after the marriage to educate him about the lady of the woods and their ways. "Do it in stages," her momma told her.

"Only tell him what is absolutely necessary if you know what's good for you," her Grandma Rosemary suggested.

Her Yanyo had always marched to the beat of her own drum. "Tell him everything, every sordid little detail. We need to see what this fiancé of yours is made of, see if he's built to handle it." If it was up to Yanyo Rose, she would've began disclosing their secrets the night he proposed.

When she told him the Lady of the Woods was real, he didn't flinch. She explained she'd have to visit her every morning once she took over the inn. He interpreted it in his own way. "I believe in ghosts. A property steeped in history like the grounds at Ravenwood is sure to have them."

The lady wasn't a ghost. Although, Lucinda wouldn't quite describe her as a person either. Once Timothy met her, he would understand, but she couldn't bring him into the clearing until he was invited.

It never came to pass. The lady didn't seem concerned with making his acquaintance. Maybe after all the decades of disastrous husbands, she had given up on them entirely.

Timothy thought the trees weren't judged fairly. He had a different theory about the evil forces which lurked there. He thought the fear of the legends so many brought with them to the woods brought on the tragic events. The negativity of the trees needed to be replaced with love and light. Then the bad luck that surrounded Ravenwood would melt away.

"Nobody's perfect." Her mom told her in private after learning about Timothy's new age view of the property. "We all knew he had to have a flaw."

It didn't sit right with Lucinda. On the one hand, her mom was right, but it was only because Timothy hadn't learned the truth yet for himself. Once he met the lady, once he experienced some of the off the cuff events which occurred inside the property, he'd come to see the place for what it was. Ravenwood was a home for evil. Lucinda was a Weaver woman which meant Timothy, as her husband, was another in a long line of stewards of darkness.

He surprised everyone with his courage, or stupidity depending on who you asked, by venturing off into the trees on multiple occasions. The part that was so shocking was his return. Every single time.

The first time he did it Lucinda was beside herself in fear. She had begged him not to do it, tried to warn him of the dangers, but he went anyway. She paced the grounds and searched the trees from the trail, calling out to him without an answer. The woods were kind to the Weaver women, and she could've gone after him. Everyone's kindness has a limit, and she figured these woods were no different. She wasn't going after anyone who might already be on the receiving end of Ravenwood's wrath, husband or not.

After that, he didn't announce his little adventures. He'd slip off unnoticed. Lucinda did her best to keep an eye on him, hoping to stop him if she saw him headed that way. It became a full time job in itself, much harder than running after a child she would learn soon enough. Once she noticed he was gone, she was useless to get anything done until he returned.

The pregnancy changed his behavior for a little while. He reluctantly agreed not to go exploring until after the baby came, but he insisted she was worried about nothing. She had hoped once their daughter was born he'd continue to stay close to the inn for their baby's sake.

Timothy was filled with stories about his little experiments and how he believed they were working. Positivity was the answer. There were recordings he'd bring with him of motivational speeches and uplifting sayings which he'd play for the trees. He'd talk to the trees, complimenting them, thanking them for the work they did for the property and the environment. The leaves would flip over, branches would sway near him and nowhere else. The trees seemed to lean in closer to him. These were all signs the woods were responding the way he'd hoped.

"They're leaning closer because they're ready to reach out and grab you if you don't stop this nonsense." Lucinda snapped at him during a middle of the night feeding when she could barely keep her eyes open. If he wasn't going to help with little Lorelei, he might as well go back to sleep.

He wanted others to come with him. The work he was doing, and yes, he considered it his job at the inn, was paying off, but the time frame was too slow. If he had a group of people with him, they could send out the positive vibes en masse. It'd create a larger domino effect. He believed eventually the trees he helped would send out the positive energy themselves, so it would be beneficial to have a group kick start the process. The only real argument they ever had was when Lucinda refused to force any existing employee to help him, or create new job titles and hire people for this sole purpose.

Just as she always feared, the day came when he didn't return from one of his excursions. It'd been a long time since she'd watched him like a hawk, so she hadn't realized he'd gone. There was a baby who took priority. It was a feeling she couldn't explain. Something came over her while rocking Lorelei to sleep for her afternoon nap, and she just knew. This was Timothy's last trip to the woods.

Lucinda checked around the inn first without raising anyone's suspicions. Morose had been her style for so long before he came into her life that no one really thought twice when it suddenly crept up on her again. With every place she checked, the feeling in her chest grew stronger. He wasn't in the grand hall, or the office, not in the break room or kitchen. She checked the garage, but didn't find him. Their car was there, so wherever he was, he went on foot. The gardens were empty.

With a broken spirit, she stood in front of the trail entrance and willed her feet to move, but they didn't listen.

It wasn't because the morning rain had turned the dirt path into a muddy mess. It wasn't because she worried about finding her husband's body hanging from a tree by the rope used as a hindrance to keep people on the path which did very little to deter guests from doing whatever they wanted.

It was because she knew she wouldn't find anything. There'd be no trace of Timothy until the woods wanted her to find something. If the trees were ready to disclose the identity of the latest notch in their bark, they would do it whether she stepped foot on the trail or not.

This was an agony so many of the women in the family had already lived through. It would take a long time for a missing person to be declared dead. She'd be married to a ghost until then. There'd never be a body, never any closure. As much as she understood the trees murdered her husband, she'd never be able to distinguish that little spark of hope she was wrong.

Maybe he'd be one of those people who was transported down the road or out of state. Maybe he'd magically walk out of the woods years from now not realizing how much time had passed. Maybe he had a mistress in Appleton and ran off with her. Anything was better than the other thoughts, the more realistic ones, the thoughts Lucinda was doing her Lamaze to breathe through while she tried to bury them.

When she came through the inn, she stopped at the reception desk. "Hey, Alice," she said, trying to keep the sound of her broken heart out of her voice. "Have you seen Timothy?"

"No, ma'am," Alice said sweetly. "Is he supposed to be around?"

Lucinda shook her head and waved her hand, dismissing

the question. "Oh, you know Tim." She did her best to smile, but it made the hurt she was swallowing rise up faster.

Alice smiled awkwardly darting her eyes away. Her husband's excursions into the woods were a wide spread source of gossip at the inn. Alice stayed out of most of the nonsense, but she surely heard some of the talk.

"If you see him," Lucinda said, but didn't finish the sentence. *'No one will ever see him again.'*

"You want me to give him a message?"

Lucinda shook her head. "I'm going to lay down while Lorelei's napping, and I don't want to be disturbed. That's all."

"Certainly. Rough night?" Alice asked. "I'm sorry. I thought she was sleeping better."

"She's cutting teeth again," Lucinda said before slowly walking up the stairs. She laid in her bed facing the window, watching the tops of the trees sway gently in the wind. One of them was responsible for her husband's fate, and she wondered which it was. *'Are there any trees left who are innocent?'*

The tears which she could feel trying to break free since she first had the sensation Timothy was gone never came. Now that she was alone in her room, save from her sleeping child, there was no urge to cry. It's inconceivable to grow up a Weaver and not be prepared for heartache. The years of misery spent wallowing in pity over what misfortunes she would one day face used enough of the resources she had for sorrow to make grieving an impossibility.

By the time she went to bed that night, everyone knew, but no one was talking about it at least not around Lucinda. There was an uncomfortable silence in every room she walked into which only added to her sadness. Still, her tears remained at bay.

There was simply a return to the former way of things. The loss of Timothy shifted her back to her old self. The only difference between the Lucinda people saw after he disappeared, and the one they had known before she met him was her memories of a brief window when she was happy. Those memories seemed fake, like images from a movie she had watched a lifetime ago.

'It's the hope,' she thought. *'I might know he's gone, but until there's proof, there will always be a small part of me hoping to see him walk through the door whether I feel that spark of light or not.'*

The next morning, she was awakened early by Yanyo Rose. "Come child. Let's see the lady together."

Yanyo still went to the clearing every day even though her service ended. She took Lorelei almost every single morning when the weather permitted.

"I don't feel like it," Lucinda said, rolling over away from her. The inn wasn't officially hers yet. The morning treks through the woods weren't her responsibility, and right now, the woods were the last thing she wanted to be near.

"We can talk to the lady about Timothy," Yanyo told her. "She'll know what happened."

Lucinda sat up and faced her. "She definitely knows what happened! That doesn't mean she'll share the news with us."

Yanyo nodded her head slowly and shifted Lorelei to her other side. "You're right, but it's worth trying," she said. Rozalia walked to the bedroom door. "And you're coming," she said without looking back. "I'll be in the kitchen. Don't make me wait long."

Lucinda flopped onto her stomach, burying her face into a pillow. Her screams were muffled, and she kicked and punched her bed. A few moments later she inched her way to the edge and threw the covers off her. It was no use. Yanyo Rose always got her way.

She did make Yanyo wait, however. It had been a long time since someone drug her to the clearing. It was only appropriate she look her best for her reintroduction to the lady. If anyone was sent to check on her, they'd see she was getting ready to leave. "Appearances are important, and one should take effort to look their best." That's what her mother had always told her.

The hot water in the shower was barely running luke warm by the time she stepped out. She went through her entire skin care routine at a painstakingly slow pace. The outfit she picked out wasn't exactly sloppy, but it was suitable for a hike. Most of her clothes didn't fit right since having a baby even though she lost all the weight in the first month. She had to change her clothes three times before finding something that fit.

Applying a full face of makeup wasn't necessary especially since most days she skated by with lip gloss and mascara. There wasn't enough time to get it done in between bouts where Lorelei needed her attention. Times like this when Yanyo took her in the mornings were better spent sleeping. Even so, it's what she did, hoping her great-grandmother would give up and leave before she came downstairs.

It wasn't until she was styling her hair she began to regret her delay. The woods were still the last place she wanted to be, but it was unfair to Yanyo Rose who was only trying to help. Her heart was in the right place even if her methods weren't ideal.

'No one has come to see what's taking so long. She's given up and gone on without me.'

Missing out on going to the clearing didn't break her heart. Looking in the mirror at the beautiful creature staring back at her less than twenty-four hours after her husband's death was soul crushing. She should've never made herself up to this extent.

She slipped on her shoes and went downstairs quietly greeting Alice when she passed the reception desk. Alice did a double take when she saw her. *'Probably doesn't remember a time when I took this much effort,'* she thought. *'Probably curious why I chose now to do it.'*

As she approached the kitchen, she could hear Yanyo Rose's voice drifting down the hall. She was singing to Lorelei. *'They're already back? Strange. How much time did I take?'*

"Perfect," Yanyo said when she entered the kitchen. "You're right on time." Yanyo scooped up Lorelei and headed to the back door, pausing to wait for Lucinda.

She followed Yanyo out the door and through the garden. The trail entrance was as far as she'd go. It was ridiculous to expect her to go into the woods so soon.

Yanyo Rose peered back at her every few seconds, checking that Lucinda was still behind her. When they reached the trail, she stopped. "You can't let them beat you too," she said. "Come."

Lucinda closed her eyes for the first few steps then kept her eyes glued to the dirt path they called a walking trail. She didn't want to see the trees. She didn't want to imagine what they were thinking. *'Do they pity me? Do they feel any remorse over taking my child's father from her? Or are they laughing at me?'* A breeze picked up, shaking the branches of the trees around them, making a quiet rustling sound. *'I suppose there's my answer.'*

When they reached the part of the trail where they'd veer off to head to the clearing, Lucinda slowed her pace. Once Yanyo Rose was in the woods, she'd continue on the trail to the other side of the gardens. Her Yanyo stopped on the trail and waited.

"We must see the lady," Yanyo told her.

Lucinda's head jerked up, and she shook her head. *'Unbelievable.'*

"We must see her before she seeks you out."

The lady could reach her anywhere. Chances were she wouldn't even show in the clearing this morning. If she wanted to see Lucinda, this was the best way. She nodded at her Yanyo and followed her off the trail toward the stairs.

It was more difficult for Lucinda to manage the rest of the hike. Yanyo could do it blindfolded with both hands tied behind her back. She practically lived in the clearing. Lucinda could find her way without direction, but her movement was slow and filled with apprehension. One wrong step and she'd find herself at the bottom of the ravine, the latest victim of Ravenwood.

Yanyo Rose had gone on ahead and was waiting with Lorelei where the well-worn trail in the ravine wall had been walked into existence. Her daughter was sitting in the grass laughing and swaying her body back and forth to the songs Yanyo was singing. The words were Hungarian, but Lucinda could sing them by heart even if she wasn't sure what the words meant.

When she caught up to them, Yanyo lifted Lorelei into the air and spun her around. No one would believe the woman was over a hundred years old. The pearls of laughter ringing out from her daughter made the morning feel right for a moment. Then her reality rushed back, and she sighed.

Yanyo heard it and brought Lorelei to her hip, holding her as she had the entire walk. "It's almost over," she said quietly. "We'll know right away if there will be answers today, and then you may go ahead on back while we stay and rejuvenate."

'Hope.' Lucinda thought as she turned into the opening in the ravine wall leading to the clearing. *'It's a dangerous thing.'*

She watched her Yanyo set Lorelei on the ground in the clearing ahead of her. The two of them held a special bond. Before walking through the wall of trees to join them, Lucinda looked up at the bright blue sky knowing the trees would soon twist together, blocking it from view.

When she did, she dropped to her knees and screamed. Yanyo came running for her, but the branches began to grow and wrap around each other, folding in over the clearing, essentially trapping Yanyo Rose and Lorelei inside, barricading Lucinda from entering. The watch could still be seen fastened around a branch not far from where sat silently sobbing. It was the watch she gifted her husband on their first anniversary.

Chapter Sixteen

Spoiled Apples

There were two types of people who came to the church. Some of them recognized free will wasn't a scape goat. A person could make their own choices, but the responsibility behind it was to do the right thing. The hope was each person would exercise their free will to do what the Lord wanted them to do, and in a nut shell, the Lord demanded respect.

We are only vessels here, mere pebbles in the landscape of eternity. The Lord fashioned our bodies, and we needed to care for them, not abuse ourselves with drugs, whatever junk we could eat, and marring ourselves with tattoos and piercings. This entire universe was created by God, yet so many do nothing but work toward its destruction. The planet wasn't a gift given to his children for them to play rough with and break it two weeks later because in the context of all of time, our days are shorter than we think.

And, of course, we must worship him. Thank him. Praise him. We must constantly show him our eternal love by living right. That's how we show our respect.

Then there were those who saw church as a safety net. It was a get out of hell free card, and she despised them for making a mockery of the teachings of the Lord. The hate she felt for them was her biggest flaw, and if anything kept her from the glory of heaven, that was going to be it.

Forgiveness is for the weak. It's for those who would use it as a crutch. They think they can do anything they want because all they have to do is ask forgiveness, and all their sins will be washed away. Yes, it was true, but that doesn't mean it was intended for anyone to take advantage of it.

Margaret preached to her congregation that was also a sin. Twisting the Lord's word to the advantage of the fair weather believer would not go unpunished. If someone were to steal from their employer and ask forgiveness, the Lord would grant it. If they continued to steal, lie, cheat, or any of a number of other despicable actions and ask forgiveness, the Lord would grant it.

Do any of them ever ask forgiveness for abusing the Lord's grace? No, of course not. They think they're smarter than the Lord. They believe they found a loop hole. Their initial acts will be forgiven, but not the shadiness behind their methods. If they figure it out and ask forgiveness for that too, it's another sin.

"The point is," Margaret hissed to the nineteen people sitting in her basement. "The road to the kingdom of heaven is not paved with good intentions!"

"Amen," several in the audience agreed.

"There is no entry into blessed eternity by picking and choosing."

"Amen."

"The gates will not open if you've been busy finding a way to get around the parts you don't want to adhere to."

"Amen." More were joining in now.

"Living right by the Lord is living by his word, not running amok without care, thinking forgiveness alone will be the answer to save your soul."

"Amen!"

Asking for forgiveness when you come to find God was meant to be a clean slate. *'You were lost, but now you're found.'* After that, there needs to be more than words. If the actions to do better, to be better aren't visible after that prayer request, than there will be a shocking revelation come judgment day.

While she spoke, she watched the man sitting in the back row of folding chairs stand and walk up the stairs. The urge to call him out, to bring everyone's eyes on him was strong, but she resisted. She was on hour five of her sermon. It was not uncommon for people to step out to use the facilities, but this man was on his way home.

How did she know? Because she'd seen it before. Too many times newcomers came wowed by the simplicity, the common sense of their beliefs. It was a religion and a lifestyle unlike anything they had seen. It was harder for them. Most were used to sermons lasting an hour, if that. They were used to church ending when they went to brunch Sunday morning.

So they took their time. They left when they wanted during the sermon because they were hungry. God sent his son to sacrifice everything for us, but they couldn't handle sacrificing a meal in return. Margaret suffered them in silence. It was not her place to pass judgement, and she prayed for their souls like the good Christian woman she was, had always been.

Week after week, they'd show up. Sometimes taking a Sunday off because apparently they believed God didn't take attendance. They'd hang around until they felt like leaving as though the sermon had open hours. Sometimes, they'd slowly stop coming. Other times, they gradually built up their commitment, became more driven. Then once they learned the amount of work involved, they'd bail for good.

Very few stuck around for the long haul. Of the eighteen remaining in front of her, twelve were family. Two of the other six were dating her grandchildren. Sex before marriage in all forms, including hand holding and flirting, was expressly forbidden. *'Oh, they put on a good show pretending to be friends, classmates, but I'm not so naïve I can't see through their ruse. God isn't fooled either.'*

They began with nineteen today, but one day it would be ninety. The barn would have to suffice to hold everyone when they grew. And, one day, she'd have her very own church constructed. They would continue to grow long after her days were over. They would spread their message, ridding the world of the evil overtaking every person. Once nature had nothing left to satiate its hunger, they'd have won.

Until then, she'd complete her work one lost soul at a time. If she couldn't save him, she'd dispose of him. No one puts a spoiled apple in the basket with the good ones. People should not be treated any differently.

It was three weeks before the man returned again. Margaret wasn't delivering the sermon that day. Her son Jack was at the pulpit. This church was a culmination of her life's work. Nothing brought her more joy than standing in front of her congregation regardless of how small, preaching the word of God, conveying his message as a reminder to those washed in the faith and to educate those new to Trinity Worship Springs Eternal Faith.

It was time to pass the torch to her son. They say children

are the future, and he was proof. He would take what she built further than she ever dreamed. He was genuine and charismatic. People were drawn to him like moths to the porch zapper.

After a couple weeks with him at the microphone, their numbers almost doubled. The stragglers who had made their way through the door for his first sermon spoke highly of it to others, drawing in more people. Margaret didn't feel defeat; this wasn't a competition. It was the natural order of things. Future generations were supposed to pick up where their parents and grandparents left off, doing more than they could ever dream.

She'd been in the hospital that first Sunday. Caught her foot on an icy step and tumbled to the ground snapping her ankle. If it was entirely up to her, she'd have waited until Monday to see the doctor. Pain was no excuse to miss service. Jack assured her someone would record it in its entirety and bring the tapes to her, so she could listen from her hospital bed.

The recordings played all night with her foot hanging from a makeshift stirrup tied to a metal rod above the bed. Her shouts of, "Amen!" and, "Praise the Lord!" brought the nurses running to her room several times thinking she was in distress.

"Quite the contrary," she told them. "I am filled with the Lord's love. Nothing could be more peaceful." Once wasn't enough. The sermon was so powerful, so eloquent that she had to listen again and again. Shortly before dawn, she finally fell asleep with her grandson's voice booming from the tape player on her bedside tray.

In the early morning hours, the doctor brought her discharge paperwork. *Strange,* she thought. After the surgery on Saturday to set her ankle, she was told she'd have to stay at least a week.

During the next week, they worked on a sermon together at Jack's insistence. "I just worry about you, mom. What if the pain becomes too much for you?"

"Oh, pish-posh," Margaret scoffed. "There is no pain on earth greater than being unable to reach these wayward souls. If I'm able to live each day carrying that in my heart, I think I can manage this week's service."

However, when everyone piled into the basement Sunday morning, more chairs had to be carried down from upstairs. Her son-in-law made a trip home to grab even more. Everyone who attended the previous week had returned as well as fourteen first timers. It was the biggest turn out they'd ever had. She wasn't so arrogant to not give credit where credit was due. These people were here because her son spoke the gospel in a way that captivated people's attention.

"It's time," she told him. "This is the sign I was waiting for to show me we're ready."

This was why a week later when the man who signed the registry only as "Jason" made his second appearance, she was able to follow him out when he bailed on the service. Before she left her seat, she tapped the shoulder of the young girl sitting next to her and motioned for her to follow.

The young woman was visiting her daughter for a little while. Margaret didn't approve. It was a blessing anytime they could teach the fundamentals of their church to someone new, and that was how she reconciled this visitor in her mind. Nothing about this stranger, or the logic behind her visit, sat right with her. She was hear for a specific reason, and Margaret felt it was up to her to provide it since no one else was making a move to do it.

Jason was already out the back door at the top of the basement stairs by the time Margaret made it to the top. The door to the kitchen was locked. She knew enough of the world not to put it past someone to rob them while a church service was in progress under their feet.

"Excuse me," she said, moving as fast as she could on a broken ankle. "Jason!"

He was already to his car and had opened the door when she caught his attention. He glanced at her then at his front seat and hesitated. For a moment, she was afraid he might go ahead and leave, ignoring her. Finally, he shut the door and walked across the side lawn in her direction. "Yes, ma'am," he said.

'So polite,' Margaret smiled. *'Refreshing.'*

"Thank you," she said to him. "I was hoping to make your acquaintance. I've seen you here before, but you didn't stay to the end. Just like today," she added.

"Uh, yeah," he said, scratching the back of his head. His eyes fell on the young woman standing behind her before going back to Margaret. "It's just a lot."

She showed the whites of her eyes and pursed her lips, holding back the words she longed to say. "A lot? How so?'

He shifted his weight nervously. "Well, how long do these sermons typically last?"

"One went until after seven at night," the young woman said.

Margaret shot her a look that said those better be the last words she spoke to this man. "We are passionate," she told him.

Jason explained how it was so much more than what he was used to at his last church before he moved to Massachusetts. He wasn't sure if it was the right fit. "To be honest, I think part of the extreme nature might be because it's a familial church. It might be why you're not growing."

The words Margaret heard were quite different. She heard a man whining because worship wasn't convenient. Faith in the Lord wasn't about convenience. "Give me one chance," she asked sweetly. "Come out Saturday, and I'll show you the plans for the church. We'll talk."

He reluctantly agreed. Margaret kept the faith every day he'd show for their scheduled meeting.

When Saturday morning rolled around, Margaret surprised everyone by showing up at her daughter's house unannounced. The family went into a panicked frenzy cleaning as much as possible as soon as her car pulled into the driveway. Nothing was ever good enough for her.

She nodded approvingly at her daughter and grandchildren with a smile. Something had put her in good spirits, and her family were equal parts worried and relieved. Mandy was the only one missing, having moved to California. Margaret didn't notice. Out of sight, out of mind. In fact, she barely thought about her youngest grandchild since she left the state.

"I believe we have important matters to tend to today," she said to the visitor after the routine greetings were out of the way.

The young woman smiled weakly and went to the door to slip on her shoes, leaving Margaret to offer an explanation regarding what they were off to do. The family was quite shocked to learn about their plans, but mostly grateful it was her as opposed to one of them. She hadn't mentioned it once since the church service, hoping Mrs. Sullivan would forget or the plans would get cancelled. She was terrified of the family matriarch and dreaded spending time alone with her.

It was a short drive to the area on the west end of Margaret's property which had been cleared for a hundred yards in all directions to build the church. There was a lone rundown trailer on the land now and nothing more. A few trees had to be removed and the ground leveled before construction could begin. That work had been completed in the fall before the arrival of freezing temperatures. The crew would return when the weather broke in the spring.

"It fills me with such joy to see this place," Margaret said, pulling off the road onto the hardened dirt covered land. "Soon we'll be able to reach more people with the good word. Soon." She beamed at the location of the future church, picturing the finished building in her mind. "But," she said, looking at the young woman, "it's not my accomplishment. God, himself, saw to it we'd achieve this."

They got out of the car and went inside the trailer. It protected them from the sting of the bitter cold winds, but did little else to provide comfort. The young woman rubbed her hands together, wishing she'd remembered to put her gloves back in her coat pockets yesterday.

"Do you know why you were sent to us?" Margaret asked.

The woman nodded, expecting Mrs. Sullivan to continue. "Do you?" she asked when she didn't.

"Yes," Margaret said sharply.

Twenty minutes passed. Then twenty turned into thirty.

The two of them waited inside the trailer in silence. When Mrs. Sullivan collected her so early, she thought there was more to do than simply wait, but she had been wrong. "Do you think you'll persuade him?" she asked.

"Persuade him? Whatever do you mean?" Margaret furrowed her brows together confused.

"Well to give Trinity a... To give Trinity Worship Springs Eternal Faith a chance." She corrected herself when she saw Mrs. Sullivan wince at the abbreviated name.

Margaret didn't answer right away. She stared at the blueprints for the church near a drawing of how it would look once it was built. The smile which spread across her face appeared genuine and warm which was a rare sight to see.

"I think it's wonderful after all you've been through you still have a childlike innocence," she answered. "No, child, I don't think I'll persuade him."

"Yet you do it anyway because you have hope," the woman nodded, believing she was right.

The look Mrs. Sullivan gave her made her skin crawl and her stomach flip. "That's not what today is about," she said. "Today," she inhaled deeply, "is about weeding the garden."

"Weeding?" The woman was confused. "Garden?"

"Yes, one weed could take over the entire plot if you're not careful. Someone like this Jason." Margaret hissed his name like it was venomous on her lips. "His willy-nilly non-committal ways could influence others. We're going to make sure that doesn't happen."

The young woman didn't have time to process the idea they were going to discourage him from being a more active member of the church. The sound of an engine grew closer until a car pulled in next to Mrs. Sullivan's. When the car door closed, Mrs. Sullivan went to the door of the trailer and greeted him warmly.

She brought the man inside and touted the church to best of her ability. She sang the praises of their charity work, their reach in the community, and what they hoped to accomplish in the future. The designs were laid out for him to look over, and she described in great detail what it would be like when everything pulled together in the end.

"I don't know," he said. "It sounds great, but like I said… It's a lot."

Margaret nodded at him and flashed the smile she used when she couldn't speak what was on her mind. "I understand. Can't blame me for trying." Margaret laughed nervously. "Well, I suppose I shouldn't keep you," she said, leading him to the door. "We've got a bit of business to tend to before leaving, but thank you so much for dropping by."

She opened the door as she spoke, and Jason stepped through it without looking while saying his goodbyes. Instead of the wooden stairs, his foot met empty air, and he fell to the ground with a thud.

"What the hell?" he moaned, rolling over and applying pressure to his lower back.

"Something like that," Margaret said, closing the door tight.

He yelled for them, then at them for a few minutes. The wind picked up around them outside, and made the young woman fear there was a rare winter tornado passing through the western side of Massachusetts. Then it stopped suddenly and without warning.

"What was that?" the young woman asked.

"What was what?" Mrs. Sullivan countered. "It was wind."

"No. When you opened the door..." The young woman felt like she was trapped and cowering in her own body. All of her was curled up inside her chest while the rest of her body continued to work on its own. "I know I saw trees just outside."

"Trees?" Mrs. Sullivan asked. "Are you sure?"

The woman nodded, and with tears in her eyes added, "And a castle in the distance."

Chapter Seventeen

Twin Bond

'*It's going to be fine. I just have to lay low for a few days until this whole thing blows over,*' he said to himself, staring in the distance at the ravine.

Roger didn't necessarily believe in the tales the people around town endlessly told about the woods east of Appleton, but he wasn't going to test it out either. The ravine was part of the property. That much he knew for sure. Where the line between Ravenwood and Moss Farms was drawn wasn't as clear. About twenty yards from the ravine is what he'd heard, so staying at least fifty yards away was his safety net.

He should've known his brother was up to no good. All his life he had only wished for one thing: a brother. One who was better than the one he had anyway. They were twins for heaven's sake! All this nonsense about a twin bond was so called professionals blowing smoke. Oh, sure, he felt it when something happened to his brother. The day his brother got arrested in New Hampshire for breaking and entering was one of the worst days of his life. He spent the day in a fear driven panic not sure where his paranoia was coming from until Ray used his one phone call on him.

For the last twenty years, he'd been trying to distance himself from his brother. Ray made his childhood miserable.

The apple doesn't fall far from the tree, right? Well, if one apple is bad, it must mean the whole bushel is rotten. Every teacher treated him like he was no better than Ray. Whenever something happened, a kid was whispering when they should've been working, something was broken or missing, Roger was blamed. He must be just like his brother.

No one in their hometown would hire him. Ray already had a reputation as a thief, getting caught taking stuff from the store using the five finger discount. He stole from his friends, their parents, everywhere he went he took something. It was like an addiction.

When Roger met Helen, they settled down in the next state far from Ray's reputation. Their life had been so good. His worst day there was better than his best day living in his brother's shadow.

Ray broke into a home in Virginia not realizing the owner was the chief of police. The headlines made it all the way to Delaware. Somehow the local news found out he was Ray's brother, and it was like his childhood all over again. His boss eyed him suspiciously every morning when he came to work. Started asking him questions about the amount of supplies he was going through and if he knew where certain items were because they seemed to be lost.

'Because if I'm going to steal, a box of a hundred paper clips is on the top of my list,' he shook his head.

He sat down on the ground, resting against a tree, nervously checking over his shoulder every few seconds that the ravine was far in the distance. The pillow case Helen had haphazardly thrown a few items into sat between his feet. There were assorted cans of beans and soup, a can opener, one spoon, and a roll of toilet paper. He laughed. *'Helen always thinks of everything.'* He placed each of the cans in front of him, and his fingers touched something else. It was a Payday bar, his favorite.

'Well, this and the two jugs of water need to last until Friday morning.' He'd been so against buying the plastic jugs of milk from the store, wanting to keep the daily deliveries. The prices in Appleton were too high. He'd taken a pay cut to move there after the trouble his brother caused for him from his crimes in Virginia. Those empty jugs were a lifesaver today.

He checked over his shoulder again. It was still there. The ravine was right where he left it. The one thing he wished he'd thought to bring was a pillow. The days were warm, and he grabbed a jacket on the way out of the house in case it got chilly at night. It could double as a blanket. *'Three days,'* he thought to himself. *'At the most.'*

The sound of his stomach growling was distracting him, but he didn't want to eat anything too quickly. It had to last. He could hear the sound of Helen honking from the road in a matter of hours, or it might not be till Friday morning when they agreed she'd collect him regardless. Always err on the side of caution. He had to assume he'd be here the whole time.

Roger should've stopped and grabbed a bite after the job interview in Barre. It had been the plan since he left the house, but he was in a hurry to get home. His brother was up to something, and he feared the worst. He was right.

A couple more hours passed with Roger having nothing to pass the time except keep track of the seconds ticking off on his watch and checking on the ravine. He gave in to his hunger and ate an entire can of beans too fast. His stomach barely noticed what he swallowed, demanding more.

The sun was moving overhead, and the shadows it cast chilled him. There was an open area not far away where the beams still shone down through the treetops to the ground. It was closer to the ravine, and he was afraid to move. When his shivering neared almost constant, he packed up and started walking. The ground would be warmer there for sleeping too he decided. He stopped more than once to survey the distance. The ravine was still plenty far enough away.

He situated himself just off the middle where he knew the rays of warmth would extend the longest and laid down. It was still hours till the time he typically went to bed, but there was nothing else to do out here. Sleep, if he could manage it, would make the time pass quicker. *'Hopefully, the horn will wake me up.'*

When he woke, it was pitch black all around him. No light from the night sky made it through the trees. *'A flashlight,'* he thought. *'That and a blanket is what I forgot.'*

His teeth rattled from the crisp air, and he sat against the nearest tree. The sun needed to hurry back. He couldn't see the face of his watch to estimate how long he had to wait.

'How could I have been so stupid?' he yelled at himself again.

They hadn't even been in Appleton a full year when Ray tracked them down. He should've been in prison. It would've been for good too seeing as how breaking into that sheriff's home violated his parole. It was a comedy of errors which led to his supposed innocence. Some of the evidence had been mishandled, but there would've been more than enough to lock him away. The prosecution botched the case, and his brother was turned loose on society again.

"How did you find me?" he asked, bewildered to see Ray on his porch.

"It wasn't easy," Ray said. "Clara gave me the address."

"Clara! You bothered my daughter?" He had missed a call from her at work yesterday. His secretary took the message, but he had a late meeting and forgot to call her back. This must be why she was trying to get ahold of him.

"What do you mean bothered? Can't an uncle visit his niece?"

Those words angered him. He'd never been an uncle to anyone. "What do you want, Ray?"

His brother acted hurt, ready to play off the sweet, just here to visit act, but the stare down from Roger stopped him. "Fine. I'll level with you. I need a favor."

"I don't have any money," Roger said, stepping back to shut the front door.

"Ouch!" Roy slid his foot against the frame, keeping the door from shutting. "It's not money. I promise."

Roger wouldn't let him in the house. He knew better. Helen would be noticing things missing for weeks if he had. But, he did come outside to hear his brother out.

There was a job in Barre, a good one. It was at a trucking company, and they hired people like Ray, people with a past.

"What do you need from me?" Roger asked. "A ride?"

"Listen. I was hoping you'd go to the interview for me."

Roger laughed and ran his fingers through the back of his hair. *That's Ray for you. When he isn't getting in trouble, he's good for a joke.*

"Oh, wait," he said, seeing the look on his brother's face. "You're serious?"

"I'm not good in these situations. C'mon! You know that. This could be really good for me. It's the first time I've been able to see a future for me that didn't include bars. But... I know I'm gonna mess it up like I always do. Say the wrong thing."

It took a lot more convincing, but Roger finally agreed to take the following Tuesday off to land his brother this job. Anything to get Ray out of town was worth it.

The interview was probably one of the best ones Roger ever had. It wasn't till the end he realized his brother set him up. "So," he asked the owner hesitantly, "when do you think I could start?'

The man narrowed his brows and said, "Monday. You know that."

It was Roger's turn to be confused.

"I already told your parole officer the job was yours," he said. "You're the one who insisted on the interview, to earn it."

The overwhelming dread that filled him with those words was like nothing he had ever felt. "Can I use your phone?" he asked.

Helen didn't answer which increased his worry. He drove across the state as fast as he could, only stopping for fuel. The one station he picked out of the dozens he had passed was the one with an out of order pay phone. He couldn't stop again. It would slow him down, and he had to get home.

The dark tint to the sky began to fade overhead into ever growing softer shades of blue as he replayed the events which got him into this mess. Eventually, he could see the time. He guessed he'd been up since around three. His watch wasn't the only thing he could see. He soon noticed the ravine was gone.

Roger jumped to his feet and looked around him in all

directions. It was gone. *'It had been right there,'* he thought. *'Or there,'* he turned around. *'A blanket, a flashlight, and a compass. Where am I?'*

He was fine though. He took a few deep breaths and thought about what to do. The rumors weren't true. It had been a long day yesterday. His brother, his hunger, his hurry to get away from the police, worrying about what Helen was being put through, everything muddied his mind. When he found the spot to sleep, it must've been away from the ravine, not toward it. Convincing himself of this was hard when his mind kept flashing still picture memories of seeing the ravine coming closer and closer as he moved through the trees.

"All that matters is I'm okay," he said out loud.

'Maybe I should just go back. I panicked. That's all. I should've never run and left everything for Helen to straighten out on her own.'

Once the sun appeared and started to move, he'd be able to figure out what direction he needed to head off to find the road. He'd go back to Appleton even if it meant getting arrested. Everything would work out. Someway, somehow, they'd be able to prove he wasn't the one who robbed the bank.

It wouldn't be easy. There were at least a dozen witnesses, people who knew him. It couldn't have been his twin brother. *'Oh, no! There's no way it was Roy. How could Roy rob the First State Bank of Appleton at 10:36 when he was in Barre for a job interview he promptly arrived to at 10:30?'*

When the rising sun showed him which direction was east, he started walking. It shouldn't take long before he ran into something familiar. He'd either hit one of the loops of Route 116 or Moss Farms. Either way, he'd be on his way to Appleton, putting the legends of Ravenwood behind him.

The longer he walked the more lost he felt. Nothing ever changed. It was more trees after trees. Twice he'd stop to eat. The hours were ticking off on his watch, but he was still in the woods. When the sun rose high overhead, he stopped to rest. It'd be easy to get turned around now. Roger didn't know what was going on, but he was starting to think those locals might've had a few things right. If that were the case, he didn't want to accidentally head off in the wrong direction.

Once the sun moved across the sky more, he kept it on the other side, still heading east. The woods were endless. He wasn't sure where he was anymore, but New York wasn't an unrealistic guess. His stomach was screaming at him for the third time today.

'That's not entirely true,' he realized. *'It never really quit after it started last night.'*

He stopped to open another can of soup when the perilousness of his situation hit him. The pillow case was much lighter because of what he already ate, even with the empty cans rattling around in it. He had about one gallon of water left, but he'd been drinking out of both containers equally. The fear of running out of food or water before finally making it out of the woods struck hard.

The trees started spinning around him. He sunk to his knees and laid down, hoping the spell would pass quickly. He concentrated on his breathing. The only way he was going to get out of this mess was by not panicking. *'Pull it together,'* he repeated silently.

Roger spread out on the ground and dozed off. He hadn't meant to fall asleep, but he felt a lot better when his eyes opened again. The sun had sank farther in the sky, but there was still enough light to cover some more distance before he wouldn't be able to see enough to continue.

His stomach was being obnoxious again, but it'd have to wait until he stopped for the day. He picked up his supplies and looked around. It seemed different, like he didn't remember being here before, but one tree had long ago began to blend into another and another until the whole of the woods was like walking in a giant circle.

Ahead of him the trees grew up close together like a hedge. This was definitely new. It made him nervous. He'd have to squeeze his way through, and the idea of it made his stomach flop. The sun still pointed him in this direction, and the tree hedge stretched on as far as he could see in both directions.

He tossed the pillow case through, then the jugs of water, and turned sideways to follow. His leg made it through fine, but his body was another story. The trees almost pressed into him more as he pushed through, tightening the space he had to move. All that was left was one arm and his head, and he was on the other side.

Roger stood on the sidewalk staring at the busy street in front of him thinking he had either died or it was a mirage. This didn't make any sense. He slowly rotated a full circle taking in the bustling business district, but behind him were only buildings. The trees he remembered barely making it through were gone.

He walked into the building closest to him, ironically a bank. He looked around at the people in line for the cashiers and wondered where on earth he was. This certainly wasn't Appleton.

A man approached him, "Good morning! Anything I can help you with today?"

Before Roger could say anything, a phone rang on a nearby desk.

"Excuse me," the man said, walking over to answer it. He motioned for Roger to follow him and have a seat.

Roger sat at the small desk across from him, still looking around in awe at how large the bank was.

"Good morning! First Financial Bank of Cincinnati. This is Stuart," the man said.

The blood drained from Roger's face, and he could feel himself turning white as a ghost. *'Cincinnati? Can't be. I did not walk that far in a day's time.'*

"Unh huh," the man said, leaning back in his chair and rotating a pencil between his fingers. "I see. I would recommend..."

The sound of his voice trailed off as the room began to haze over for Roger. He felt like he would pass out. His mouth went instantly dry, and he glanced from side to side not sure where his water jugs went.

Stuart cradled the phone. "I apologize. It's been a crazy week, and it's only Tuesday," he chuckled.

"Tuesday?" Roger asked in disbelief.

"Yep, all day," the man said. "Unless it rains!" He slapped his desk, laughing at his own joke. "Now what can I do you for?"

"What's the date?"

The man eyed Roger cautiously, but said, "It's the nineteenth."

Roger glanced at his watch. It was a quarter after ten.

"Guess I can't be robbing the bank in Appleton if I'm in Ohio," he muttered. None of this made sense. When he looked back at Stuart, his hand was on the phone, and there was an expression of panic on his face like he was about to call security.

"Sorry," he said, realizing he jumped from the frying pan into the fire. "Wrong place for that joke."

Stuart chuckled nervously, but moved his hand from the phone. "What brings you in today?"

Roger removed his ID from his wallet and slid it over to Stuart, making sure this man could provide an air tight alibi for him. "My wife and I are planning a move here from Appleton, Massachusetts," he lied. "I'm just checking out a few places, like the banks in town, to see where we want to take our business. The name's Roger. Roger Meade."

Chapter Eighteen

The Stuff Nightmares Are Made Of

The nightmares were returning. That wasn't entirely true seeing as how they never completely went away. There was always an occasional nightmare about the woods. It would be strange to work at Ravenwood and not wake up in a panic from a dream about the trees. The bad dreams had calmed down some time after she first went to work there. They only infiltrated her sleeping mind on occasion anymore.

That was until recently. For the last several weeks, they'd been increasing. Alice had gone from one or two a year to having a nightmare about the woods every week. This was her second one since Sunday, and it was only Wednesday. At least it would be in the morning when she woke up for work.

There was no more sleep for the rest of the night. Every time she tried to lay down, the shadows of her room creeped over her, and her mind envisioned the branches trying to claim her. It was going to be a long day facing the very thing which kept her awake and stole her rest.

It was the worst possible day for her to feel and look her worst. The new maintenance man had just finished his orientation, and his boss brought him around to be introduced to everyone. Alice had never wished she had warning to make sure she looked her best more in her life.

Since her split from her ex, the last thing on her mind had been another relationship. That was a road she didn't want to travel down again. Everyone tried to convince her there were better men out there, and she knew that. She just wasn't ready.

There was a sadness in this man's eyes when she first met him. Everyone here had an air of sadness around them. It takes hold the moment the job is offered and never let's go. His was different, darker somehow, like there was already something there before he came to Ravenwood, just like Alice. Whether it was actually there, or she saw it because it mirrored her, she couldn't tell.

The friendship developed first over their lunch breaks. Most people at Ravenwood preferred to take a later lunch. It made the day go by faster. Instead of an afternoon which dragged on for eternity, it helped the remaining hours of the shift fly by.

For Alice and Larry, the time they took their lunch wasn't an option. Being new on the staff, he didn't have a say. There were only two in his department, and his boss sent him to lunch when he felt like it. Mrs. Weaver sent Alice to lunch first because by the time she returned, the front desk was busier. Check in's would be arriving. The phone would be ringing with inquiries which needed to be fielded. Most of the calls weren't about room availability. They were asking for interviews, wanting a quote for an article, or hoping for permission to conduct a ghost hunt on the property. This way Mrs. Weaver wasn't the one who had to be bothered with as much of the work.

That's how they met, being the only two employees forced to take a lunch break before they were even halfway through their shift. It built slowly for her. Larry was far more outgoing than she was. He'd spend their break eating and talking nonstop. It was nice to be around someone, and she enjoyed listening to him. She just never knew what to say.

It was close to two months later before she began to open up. That was only because he was concerned about her. The dark circles under her eyes had grown ever so slowly darker day by day. After half a break of watching her eat her soup with a fork from where he sat a table away, he had to say something.

"Is there something going on at home?" he asked.

The question shocked her. It was the question she'd been asked years ago when she was suffering through abuse from her ex. She was in a better place now and had been ever since. "No," she said quietly.

"It's just that I can tell something is going on. What's bothering you?" he asked.

'Nothing,' she thought, shaking her head since he couldn't read her mind.

"If you don't want to talk to me, that's fine," he said, pushing himself away from the table. "But talk to someone, okay? I mean it."

Alice stared at him wondering why on earth he was acting like this until he made his way to her table. She was confused for a moment when she saw the spoon he was offering her. Then she looked down at the fork in her hand.

"Oh!" she cried out in embarrassment. She place her head in her hands and wished she could just vanish. Her exhaustion was so severe she hadn't noticed she wasn't actually eating anything with every bite, but simply getting a little taste of the broth.

Larry set the spoon on her table and went back to his seat. "Don't worry bout it none," he told her. "We all have our days."

She kept her face buried, refusing to look up until he was gone. Mrs. Weaver had a phone call which kept her later than usual this morning, so Alice was a little late going to lunch. There'd be enough time to finish her soup after he left. It'd have plenty of time to cool by then too. Her plan was to keep her face hidden, but then she heard him laugh.

Taking a quick peek to see if he was making fun of her, she saw him digging into a pudding cup with a fork, having just given her his spoon. Alice sat up and watched him wondering why he didn't just take his spoon back. When he saw her looking his way, he held up a fork containing barely any chocolate pudding then raised it as if to toast her. "Looks like we have something else in common," he said. "Neither of us know how to eat."

That's what started it. That's what broke the tension for her. After that, she opened up to him about her nightmares, about the trees hunting her down. They were increasing in frequency, and she was having them several times a week now. It hadn't been this bad before, not even in her early days at the inn.

Larry couldn't take her nightmares away, but he was someone who listened. She kept things like this from her family. Her parents worried, and her brother's answer was to quit. He had left the inn safely. Very few had ever managed it, but he took a job in a nearby state. The woods didn't come after him.

"Join me," he'd beg. "You can stay here while you find a place."

It was a generous offer, but she couldn't do that to Bobby.

He and his wife had just welcomed their fourth child into the world. She didn't want to be a burden and add to their stress. Besides, if she thought the nightmares were bad, sleeping in a house with four children under the age of seven would probably provide even less sleep.

They'd been dating for a couple months in secret when Alice's paranoia crept through in other ways. Every day she worried. *'What if today's the day Ravenwood splits us up for good?'*

Larry didn't share her fears at first, but as time went on, he heard more and more of the tales surrounding the property. He still wasn't exactly afraid the trees were coming for him, or anyone, but he considered it being cautious. In the end, his plan was the same as Bobby's had been.

Get away.

Make a clean exit.

Do nothing which would tempt the woods into hunting him down if that was something they were even actually capable of doing.

If he was gone from this area, he wouldn't have to worry about the trees at all. That wasn't the end of it either. He wanted Alice to come with him.

Anyone who really knew her had given up a long time ago except for Bobby. Alice wasn't going anywhere. There was a gloominess at the inn which had sunk into her skin and taken hold in her bones. It was as much a part of her now as the poor lost souls were to the trees. This was her home. It was just as terrifying as it was safe. The trees weren't going to harm her. She'd grown to trust that.

In her years at the inn, she'd become a highly treasured

member of the staff, almost family, but not quite. That was a line no one would ever be able to cross completely. She knew her place here. She knew her value. It could've been fear keeping her there, but she believed it was an understanding. They needed each other, her and the woods. The trees needed her fright to increase their strength, and she needed the protection they provided by looking after her. No one else would be able to appreciate it.

For months, Larry tried to convince her to come with him. He had a lead on first one job then another when it took too long for Alice to agree. She wasn't ready to live with him, much less move away from everything she'd ever known. And, she wasn't leaving Ravenwood.

The longer it took, the more upset he became. Their first fight was because she wanted to stay. Alice made it perfectly clear. She liked Larry and enjoyed his company, but she wasn't moving. If she went anywhere, it might be Appleton, but that was a big if. She preferred small town life, and Appleton was almost too big for her. It was nice to visit, but too noisy at night for sleeping.

Not that she got much of it anyway. The nightmares kept increasing in intensity as much as they did in regularity. She found herself dozing off at the reception desk and making silly mistakes she hadn't made since she was new to the job herself. If she kept this up, leaving or staying might not be up to her. Eventually, she was bound to mess something up bad enough for Mrs. Weaver to have no choice but to let her go.

It riled Larry up more too. The inn was no good for her, and it frustrated him that she couldn't see it. The nightmares she was having were a direct result of having to work there five days a week. Every day she took a risk by clocking in for her shift. It was never a guarantee anyone would make it home alive, but the odds were drastically against it at Ravenwood. This constant state of terror she was in, that she denied, was following her home and coming out while she slept because it had become its own monster. It had grown too large for her to keep it contained any longer.

"I'm so sorry," he said, pounding on her front door. "I didn't mean it." He stood in the rain crying after Alice kicked him out. He had told her she was too stupid to see what was right in front of her. The words came out without thinking, and he wished he could take them back. If she'd talk to him, give him a second chance, he'd be able to make her see. It was because he loved her that he worried about her so much.

Alice sunk to the floor of her kitchen, leaning against the wall, putting an extra layer of her home between her and him. She could say the same about him. He was too stupid to understand why she had to stay, but she wouldn't. After all the years of being put down, she'd never do it to anyone else.

She knew he hadn't left by the time she drug herself to bed because his car was still parked out front. He could do whatever he wanted. She was going to lay down. It would be another rough night anyway, but she needed whatever hours of sleep she could get before going to work for the last shift of the week. Hopefully she'd be able to catch up on some rest this weekend because she planned on doing nothing else but stay in bed.

When she awoke in the middle of the night, it was the same scary dream. Alice was running through the woods on the property. The trees closed in as she ran. The branches grabbed at her shoulders and scratched her face. She was escaping death repeatedly, but she was running out of energy. She had to run at full speed just to barely avoid being caught and drug down to certain death. It wouldn't be much longer before she'd run out of steam. Then it'd be over. The trees were going to win.

She felt one of the branches grip her arm and wrap an elongated bony finger around her several times. It pulled her back as she tried to continue forward. She was caught. As she fell to the ground, she tried to scream, but another branch flew into her open mouth, silencing her.

Alice flew up in bed with the scream finally flowing freely from her lips. She clutched her blanket to her chest and stared at the shadows in her room. Each was an extension of a tree at Ravenwood coming for her. There was no escaping the reach of the lady.

It took several minutes for her to calm down. Even then, she wasn't sure she was entirely out of the woods. Alice took to the floor and turned every light on, chasing the shadows which hunted her away. She paced for the rest of the night, glancing out every window she passed, looking to see if she had finally worn out her welcome at the inn.

By sunrise, she had made up her mind to leave. Larry was planning his getaway that afternoon. Once his shift was over, he was hitting the highway, leaving his forwarding address with Mrs. Weaver for his last paycheck. Alice decided to join him. If the trees wanted her, they'd find her wherever she went, but she could enjoy what little life she had left to the fullest.

It was strange Larry never stopped by to chat like she'd grown used to him doing. The morning hours dragged by slowly without one of his visits. *He must still be upset over last night.*

Lunch came and went, but there was still no sign of him. Alice was worried. Part of her hoped he was too angry still, and he was avoiding her. Deep down she didn't think that was it.

There was a lift to the mood in the castle. It was a little brighter than usual, but dark and gloomy nonetheless. When she returned to reception after her break, the door to the inn opened, and she could hear the rustling of the leaves from the woods. They were laughing.

Mrs. Weaver was about to disappear through the office door when she noticed the two uniformed police officers who had come inside. "May I help you?" she asked with a forced smile, betting their presence was about to ruin the day of everyone there.

"Morning, ma'am," said the older of the two officers. "I'm Greene, and this here's Davidson," he said, nodding to his partner who was taking in the grand hall. "We were hoping we could speak with a Lawrence Carson."

"Larry? He didn't come in today," Mrs. Weaver said.

That caught Alice's attention. She had seen him when she arrived. He was walking into the inn when she parked her car.

"That's his car in the lot, correct? Baby blue Oldsmobile?"

Mrs. Weaver was stumped. She no better knew what her employees drove than she did the names of their parents.

"Yes," Alice answered for her. "That's his car."

"So he is here?" the second officer asked Alice.

Alice noticed the irritated expression on Mrs. Weaver's face. She shrugged instead of giving a direct answer and went back to the paperwork on the counter.

"What's this about?" Mrs. Weaver asked.

The first officer thought for a moment then nodded.

"Perhaps we should talk in private."

By mid-afternoon, the news had spread throughout the inn like wildfire. Larry had been traveling up the coast running from the law. He was only a suspect in the killing of his wife, but would likely be charged with the mounting evidence against him. He had a history of mental breaks causing violence, and various police forces across the state were working together to catch him before he had another episode.

According to his boss, Larry had arrived to work on time, but in a piss poor mood. He gave him his work load for the day which included fixing one of the rope barriers on the walking trail and hadn't seen him since. The maintenance supervisor was already on his way to Mrs. Weaver's office to report Larry was missing on the job since clocking in that morning when he heard she was looking for him.

Alice heard some of the conversations drifting through the door behind her. It was obvious what everyone was thinking. The woods got to him. His body could be anywhere from the concrete floor of the boiler room to one of the many ravines. It could be discovered today, four years from now, or never. They just didn't know why the woods wanted him. It wasn't typical of the trees to attack without cause. They didn't have all the details like she did. Larry was about to take her from them, and she would've been his next victim.

Larry was never found again, but a search of his car yielded the murder weapon. It was a kitchen knife missing from the home he had shared with his wife. The blade was covered in her blood, and the handle produced perfect prints the police matched to him. They had all the evidence they needed now, but were aware it was unlikely he'd ever be seen again.

The nightmares stopped after that day. It was over a year before another random one tore Alice from her sleep in the middle of the night. The trees hadn't been coming for her. It was the exact opposite. Danger had been after her, drawing closer, and the woods wanted to warn her.

Chapter Nineteen

The Past Comes Back

The car veered off of Dunberry Road onto Route 116. Curtis leaned forward and looked around, making sure of what was obvious. "What are you doing, Mr. Howard? I thought you'd take the long route."

"Nope, that's for sissies," the driver replied. "You're not a sissy, are ya?"

Curtis gulped, but didn't answer. He sat rigid in his seat, counting his breaths as the car continued on toward Ravenwood. It was twenty minutes to Appleton, more or less depending on how fast you drove. The miles after the castle would be the longest.

This was the first time he'd ever been on this road. He had spent his entire life taken the long way around to avoid it. That's what his family had done, and he followed the unwritten rule when he got his first car. When Norma's father offered to take him to Appleton to meet a guy about a car he wanted to buy, Curtis didn't ask questions. He was just thankful for the ride and accepted on the spot without hesitation. It never occurred to him he might want to ask which route Mr. Howard would take. Everybody took the long way. There were people in dire emergencies who risked their own death by taking twice as long, if not longer, to reach the hospital in Appleton just to avoid this stretch of pavement.

His hands were trembling, and he pressed them on the tops of his legs to keep them still. He had always been intimidated by Mr. Howard. The man's presence was larger than life, looming over men others considered tall, and was off-putting at best. Norma's father looked downright scary.

Mr. Howard's wife and daughters swore he was a giant teddy bear, loving to a fault. He wouldn't hurt anybody. Unless you crossed him.

That's exactly what Curtis had done only Mr. Howard didn't know that yet.

Curtis dated Norma throughout most of high school. Her father wanted his daughters to wait before getting married instead of settling down right after graduation. He thought she should take some time to figure things out for herself about her life and her future, decide if this kid was the man who would make it happen. Live a little. It was the sixties after all. The next decade would be here before she entered her twenties. No regrets. That's all her father wanted for her.

It was all Curtis wanted as well. He'd do anything for Norma, give her anything. As far as he was concerned, he'd devote the rest of his life to make her happy.

They weren't going to wait a full year like her father wanted although they opted not to get married in June, weeks after she received her diploma like they originally planned. Their wedding date was set for the middle of October.

"What's the rush?" Mr. Howard asked when he heard the news. "Two weeks barely gives enough time to plan a reception."

Norma sweetly told him it's simply because, "I want it out

of the way before the holidays hit."

Her dad tried to convince her to wait until the spring. January would be cold and drab. Perhaps March? April would provide a nice backdrop for spring nuptials.

His daughter insisted on doing it now. She had waited this long for her father as it was. This was her wedding, her future, and she wanted it to begin.

As he watched the trees pass by the car, wondering how you could tell the differences between regular woods and the ones of Raven, Curtis worried her father suspected why they were planning their wedding in a rush. Even if he guessed it, he wouldn't have proof. Both Norma and her mom were smart enough to not let the cat out of the bag. In eight months or so when the baby comes, everyone will raise an eyebrow over the timing, but it still wouldn't prove anything.

Mr. Howard was reasoning with him to hold off on the marriage because it wasn't the best idea. He married Norma's mom right out of high school. She devoted all her energy to being the best housewife and mother she could be. She lost herself, and it took a long time for her to find her way back to the person she used to be. "I don't want that for my daughters."

"I understand. I won't let that happen to Norma," the kid tried to reassure him.

"How can you be so sure?"

The castle was on his right just ahead. The turrets peeked over the trees like giant slitted eyes watching him. There was another twelve miles to go. He was beginning to feel warm, flushed, and it was becoming harder to breathe. He hoped he'd make it to Appleton alive and in one piece.

"What's the rush?" Mr. Howard finally asked. "There's

nothing going on is there? No reason you have to marry now."

The word, "No," shook, and his voice cracked when he answered.

"So," Mr. Howard glared at him. "You can push it off a few month's then."

"She wants the wedding now," Curtis weakly replied.

"Wants it? Or has no choice?"

The kid stared straight ahead without another word. Something in the tone of the man's voice told Curtis he knew about the pregnancy. He didn't know how it was discovered, but he wasn't going to say anything. He wasn't going to admit it, and he certainly wasn't going to get caught in a lie by his future father in law.

Mr. Howard eased the car onto the shoulder and put it in park. He reached across the front seat, across Curtis and opened the glove compartment. Curtis got a whiff of the whiskey on Mr. Howard's breath when he got close. He didn't know Norma's dad had been drinking before they left.

"I found the receipt from the doctor's office," he said, removing a Revolver.

Curtis stared at the gun. The light pouring into the windshield gleamed off the metal.

"I know Norma's about to make me a grandfather."

'Run!' Curtis bolted from the car. He'd rather take his chances with Ravenwood than with Raymond "Razor Ray" Howard, undefeated Boston boxing legend.

'Mr. Howard wouldn't kill me.' His heart was pounding and sweat immediately broke out on his forehead. *'There's no way. He wouldn't kill me because he loves his daughters too much.'* There was only one place to go for any coverage. All of the

other directions left him out in the open. *'He wouldn't kill me because he wouldn't want them to go the rest of their lives without a father if he was imprisoned.'* Once his feet broke the tree line, he became paralyzed with fear.

'He wouldn't kill me because he wouldn't want his wife to not be provided for.' Curtis ducked behind the nearest, largest tree hoping Mr. Howard wasn't crazy enough to follow him into the woods. *'He won't kill me because he doesn't want his grandchild to grow up without a dad.'*

There was a brief moment of clarity when he realized Mr. Howard wouldn't do it, but he would chase him into Ravenwood hoping the trees handled the dirty work. A missing person isn't something people were typically sent to prison over unless it's proven he had something nefarious to do with it.

Curtis could barely hear his thoughts over the loud and almost painful thumping of his heart in his chest. The coolness of the shade from the trees created a dramatic decrease in atmosphere. The sweat on his brow felt cold and icy and he shivered. The chill was set deep from the start. His teeth began to chatter from the darkened temperatures of the woods and from his own fear combined. He wouldn't last for long. He was already thinking at least a gunshot would be quick.

Norma's dad could come up with any excuse and probably already had a dozen in his pocket waiting to use them. He could feed the police any reason at all for why Curtis had run into the woods. Ravenwood woods at that. He could say they had an argument over anything. *'He could say I was the one who had been drinking and stumbled to the trees to take a leak.'*

'Would Norma believe it?' The question worried him. She

was enthralled by her father, had him on a pedestal as the man she compared all men to, and wouldn't easily doubt him.

'All I have to do is wait him out,' he told himself. *'Wait him out until he leaves.'* Once he's gone, it's a quick walk down 116 until he reached the lane to the castle. He could use their phone to call for help.

For the briefest, shiniest moment, he thought he might be able to relax. His body sure made an attempt, allowing him to breathe without the effort of in-taking air and the effort of trying to do it quietly. That moment was shattered by the snapping of a twig nearby. Mr. Howard was barely several feet away.

The branches of the trees above him began to sway, and he worried he might pass out. Fight or flight kicked in, and he gave up the romantic notion of facing a bullet over Ravenwood. Curtis ran again.

Behind him, the sound of a shot rang out. Curtis studied the front of his body for emerging blood stains while carefully watching where he stepped. He didn't think he was hurt. He was too upset to know if he'd even notice. He had been wrong; this man would kill him.

That was his plan. He wasn't content with making sure Ravenwood did the trick. He was going to kill him if it was the last thing he did which is why he came into Ravenwood after him.

Curtis found another tree to hide behind. He wasn't near as fit as Mr. Howard even with his added years, even with his excessive drinking. He definitely didn't stand a chance against his gun, but he didn't have good odds against him physically in a fight. He wasn't even sure if he could outrun the old man.

He could hear Mr. Howard coming. There wasn't as much as a half-hearted attempt on his part to be quiet. He was stomping and plowing his way through the woods. "Look at all these switches," Mr. Howard yelled and laughed. "You pick one or I will."

Every noise this man made, every crack or snap Curtis heard, he worried it wasn't something on the ground. Mr. Howard was stripping branches of their leaves, pulling them back and letting them snap, making a "Whooooosh" sound that echoed through the woods. It was like he was issuing a challenge to Ravenwood that he was ready to fight.

Curtis' heart was about to give up from the strain. His equilibrium became more distorted. The palms of his hands laid flat on the trunk of the tree behind him holding him upright. The rumored lady he'd heard so many tales about would approach soon, offering him the taboo apple like they were in Eden. He'd heard she was mesmerizing, hypnotic. No one could resist her. If she offered it to him, he'd bite, sealing his own fate. If it's not her who approaches, the branches of the trees might slowly wrap around his midsection, tightening, until his body was cut in two.

His future father in law was coming closer. He sounded ten to fifteen feet off to the right. Curtis inched slowly around the tree to the left. Each movement made him dizzy and knotted his throat tighter. He continued to circle around the tree listening to every noise coming from the direction of Mr. Howard.

Once he was on the other side facing the road, he stood perfectly still while Mr. Howard continued on deeper into Ravenwood. He was almost certain he could make it to the road as long as his foot falls were light, and he was very careful. He was afraid of his future father in law seeing him.

He didn't move until he couldn't hear Mr. Howard anymore. There wasn't a single noise came from the woods except for the sound of the birds in the branches. The light rustling of the leaves in the breeze became the predominant background noise. Still he waited. Every time he thought it was safe, he told himself, *'Just a little while longer.'*

Finally he took a step. Then another. And another. With each step, he was equally trying to get away from his father in law fast in case he double backed, and he was also trying to leave the woods without becoming their prisoner. He stepped through the edge of the trees and saw the road ahead. He took off at a full sprint toward the lane, praying he made it to the castle before Mr. Howard found him.

"That little punk," Mr. Howard hissed. "You can't hide forever!"

He hadn't expected the kid to have the balls to run into the woods. That's why he drove out here: convenience. He could've shot the kid anywhere and brought his body to Ravenwood where it'd never be found. At any time, he could've pulled over and taken care of the business he set out to do. He waited until they were there because there'd be little to no risk of someone driving past at the wrong time. It was less work for him to just drag the body to the woods instead of loading and unloading him in the trunk.

He should be okay with knowing it would be taken care of one way or another. Whether it was the metal he was holding in his hand or the woods of no return, done was done. It wasn't enough. He wanted to be the one to defend his daughter's honor.

Norma was going to be fine. Once she accepted, this punk was out of her life for good, she'd go off to her aunt's in Wisconsin for a long visit while she grieved her lost love. Of course, her immediate family knew there was no aunt in the Midwest. There was a home for wayward women where she would live and be taken care of until the child was born and could be placed in an orphanage. She'd have her life ahead of her. Everything would fall into place once he took care of Curtis.

There was a noise ahead of him, and he ran toward it. "Curtis! You can't hide forever!"

Then he heard something again, but it was on his left. Mr. Howard changed direction and continued to run weaving through the woods and side swiping trees. He was going to be scratched from head to toe by the time he made it home, but his wife learned long ago not to question the marks he had.

There was the sound of coughing, and he turned back, trying to follow the noise. It echoed through the woods which made it difficult, but he was getting closer. He started walking quietly, not wanting to alert Curtis he was on to him.

The coughing came again, and he was right on top of it. There was nothing.

Another noise sounded, and he was off. He might have had a sip or two too many off his favorite bottle. He turned too quickly and started to fall, gripping a branch to steady him. The branch gave and he stumbled backward tripping on some growth which seemed to be everywhere. He managed to catch his balance before falling.

He saw movement out of the corner of his eye. *'Curtis.'*

The punk was about fifty yards away casually strutting through the trees. He took off at a fast pace and tried not to make much noise. He didn't want to startle Curtis into running again.

There was a flash of skin he recognized as an arm around a tree. *'I got him now,'* Mr. Howard thought. He'd closed about half the distance to him. *'Almost there.'*

He hurried to get closer and found him leaning against a tree. The trees were thicker here, making it appear like night was closing in when it was barely noon. "That's enough," Mr. Howard said loudly. "We both know how this is going to end."

The guy turned and looked at him.

"What?" Mr. Howard dropped a couple steps back.

It wasn't Curtis. This man looked nothing like that kid. The man in front of him looked strange. This guy's hair was longer like a woman's. His beard was unruly. The images on his hands and forearms made Raymond wonder what type of man he was dealing with because he wasn't the sort he'd typically come across after leaving the ring. Even the man's jeans were different somehow.

'Is that an earring?' Then he noticed the spikes through the man's eyebrows. Whoever he was he didn't look any more deserving to leave the woods than Curtis anyhow.

Raymond cocked the gun and aimed it at the man. "On your knees," he ordered.

The man raised his arms and looked around. He was trying to find a way out.

Raymond fired a shot into the air then took aim again. "Your knees!"

This time the man dropped to the ground, and Raymond

slowly approached him for a better look. He wouldn't have been surprised if he returned home to a news report about an escaped criminal from the penitentiary. He'd be a hero even if he couldn't claim it.

He raised the gun at him again. Judging by the man's appearance, there wasn't anyone who'd miss him anyway. It didn't matter who he was. He didn't care. Even if the guy wasn't as dangerous as he believed, he couldn't leave any witnesses who might make their way out of the woods.

Raymond cocked the gun and was about to squeeze the trigger when the man's eyes widened. *'That's right,'* he smiled. *'You should be afraid.'*

He hadn't felt the branch climb up his leg like a vine. It shot straight through his chest from the back. Mr. Howard stumbled forward, coughing, looking down in shock. His body couldn't fall. The branch was supporting him.

Another branch wrapped around his arm down to his hand. The gun fired and part of the branch shot off, falling to the ground. A cry could be heard even if only in his mind. The rest of it finished the job, completely covering him, locking the gun into his hand. Wood entered his mouth and traveled down his throat, suffocating the last of his life already leaving his body.

The other man cowered on the ground watching as the branches mummified the guy who was about to shoot him. When it finished, a tree trunk took his spot in the woods. One large branch looked like it ended with a wooden gun. There was a giant knot hole where the man's head had been, gaping open like an enormous eye staring at him.

Several men surrounded him from out of nowhere, and

the man screamed. He didn't notice their uniforms or badges before passing out on the cold forest floor.

Chapter Twenty

To Haunt Us

RATCHET WAS IN HIS room at Ravenwood watching her sleeping peacefully. He was angry, but not at her. This wasn't her fault. The experience should be enough. The castle was legit. He'd likely never stay anywhere this cool again. The breakfast they served was delicious. The grounds were beautiful especially for this time of the fall. He still couldn't help but be angry.

The lore around Ravenwood had reached Niagara. It wasn't a hot topic of conversation, but typically when ghosts or strange occurrences were mentioned, Ravenwood came into discussion. It didn't even have to get that kitche. A person could discuss their trip to Massachusetts and likely the name Ravenwood would be pulled out of someone's pocket to add to it.

He had heard it was spooky. He had heard it was haunted. He had heard there were paranormal happenings bordering on the supernatural which couldn't be explained. That's why he wanted to come here. That's why he spent the ridiculous amount of money on an overpriced room for two nights. He had hoped to encounter a ghost and have his own story to share when he went back home.

When his wife mentioned she wanted to visit an old college friend in Boston, he didn't care. She could do whatever she wanted and didn't need to ask his permission either. When she began talking about turning this visit into a shopping trip, he did groan a little bit. He should've known shopping would be on the itinerary. *'How many pairs of shoes could one woman own?'*

If it made her happy, he didn't see a problem with it. Besides if he wanted to pick on her over the seven pairs of seemingly identical black high heels in the closet – a closet he had to expand and build additional shelves just to store her shoes – she could always come back asking him how many allen wrench sets one man needed. There could only be so many 3/16 sockets he might actually have the need to hoard in the garage. The rest were just as unnecessary to her as shoes were to him.

The argument he needed them for work lost its muster years ago when so many were not just unused, but unopened. Having them made him feel better. He imagined that's how shoes affected her.

'Fine. Go. Have fun. Visit your friend. I don't care.'

Then she wanted him to come along. "Oh, Robert, a getaway for the two of us sounds amazing." She was the only person he allowed to get away with calling him by his given name, but this was pushing it.

There wasn't much he'd be able to do except maybe sit at the store and hold her purse. He wasn't interested in visiting her friend's husband whom he'd never met. He could find a local bar to pass the time away while sipping on beer and watching the Patriots play.

'No, thank you.' He'd rather sit at home in his recliner where the beer was cheaper, and the Giants were on the television.

Ravenwood was how she lured him in to the trip. "If you go, we can stop there on the way home. Stay for a couple of nights."

It wasn't something he could turn down.

He did his part. He went to Boston with his wife. He met her friend and her friend's husband. They had dinner where he made polite conversation about stuff he didn't care about, barely knew anything about. He spent one day out with his wife shopping. He sat back with her friend's husband while the women tried on outfit after outfit after outfit until his head pounded in his skull.

The next day her friend's husband had to work, so Ratchet wandered around Boston taking in a few sights. The most interesting thing he found was a local pub where the only thing anyone talked about was the Patriots and everything was wicked.

It was torture. If anyone asked, if anyone can't figure it out, it was pure torture. All of it. He counted down the hours of each day as they ticked by. Now, it was his turn. It was his part of the trip. It was his time to shine, to have a contagious smile plastered on his face, for his eyes to light up, and it was ruined.

When they arrived at the castle, there was no literature. No historical points. No signage anywhere. No pictures hanging in the hall of people who were believed to be spirits. No pamphlets on sightings. There was nothing. No mention whatsoever of the ghosts who resided here.

Bringing up the subject was also taboo. He asked the desk clerk, a sweet woman with a gentle composition. He might have well as been a ghost himself the way she reacted. She shook her head and insisted she didn't know anything. He knew it was a lie. She might be too afraid to talk about it, but that didn't mean she didn't know about it.

He was scrolling through the gardens later that day and came across a maintenance man, so he asked him. "What's the right rooms? Where's the right spots in the castle to go if someone wants to see a ghost?"

The man shifted his weight and looked around to see if anyone was close by before answering in a hushed voice. "There isn't a square inch on this property that doesn't hold the same chance as the next of something happening, but we're not allowed to discuss it."

"How's that?"

The man nodded toward the castle. "The owner doesn't like it. She doesn't like Ravenwood to have this sort of reputation. We're supposed to ignore it and hope it goes away."

He started to walk away, but stopped to add, "If you want to find something, you're on your own. None of us can help. If she catches you, if she even suspects what you're up to, she'll throw you out on the spot anytime, day or night."

Ratchet had wandered the castle and the grounds since they arrived yesterday without a single story to share. He hadn't even caught unexplained movement out of his eye, and he gets that dang near every time he hits a gas station. They'd leave tomorrow sometime after breakfast. If he was going to see anything unnatural, tonight was his last chance.

He watched his wife in her peaceful sleep of somebody whose trip wasn't ruined, wishing he could be just as content. He wasn't, and the bitterness he'd harbor over it for many years made him regret coming all the more.

Unable to sleep and feeling an overwhelming urge to do something, he stumbled down the stairs. His steps were slow, concentrated and focused. In his mind, he was pulling it off. Anyone who saw might assume he'd just woken and was a little sleepy at the most. Alcohol has that affect. Makes people think things which aren't true. If someone had seen him, they'd easily tell he was three sheets to the wind.

There was no one at the front desk. *'Perfect!'* He didn't want to be bothered by questions like he had been from the maids earlier.

He went out the front door toward the parking lot. Guests were free to come and go as they pleased. There was a quicker route through the back into the garden, but he wasn't sure if the rear doors remained unlocked all night.

When he rounded the castle to the side lot, he saw the gardens were blocked by fences. The wooden slats were over six feet tall because that's how long he loomed. The only way to the gardens was through the castle.

Ratchet leaned against the small enclosure housing the dumpsters and pulled the bottle of whiskey from his pocket. He took a swig and thought about what to do or where to head next. He'd have to try the inside door and hope he didn't run into anybody.

When he stepped away, the large swinging door to the trash enclosure inched open. Someone had forgot to put the padlock on it. This was his lucky day.

He pulled it open enough to slip through and shut it behind him. He climbed onto a dumpster nearest the fence and pulled himself over it to the gardens. His balance wasn't as stable as he believed and fell to the ground on the other side landing on his back, laying there for several minutes waiting for the pain to subside. His back ached, and his ankle felt like it would be problematic in the morning.

"That's a tomorrow problem," he muttered, slowly getting to his feet.

He pushed his way through the bushes he fell into and made it to the main paths of the gardens, heading to the other side toward where the walking trail entrance was located. If there were cameras, if anyone was monitoring them, they didn't seem too concerned about the guest who managed to make his way to the trail.

At the entrance was a large sign listing the trail rules. He stared at them, well the first one. "Trail hours are 8am to 4pm." Seemed strange to close the trail so early. It sparked his curiosity why the owners didn't want anyone in the woods after dark. It was well past midnight, but there was nothing preventing him from using the trail. Nothing except a sign guests were supposed to honor.

A small chain was pulled across with a "Closed" sign hanging from it. He could step over it as easily as he could unhook it. Lifting his foot proved a hard task, so he unlatched the chain, letting it fall to the ground. He looked around to see if anyone was in sight. Maybe someone was coming after seeing him on the security monitor after all, or maybe someone heard the chain clink and clang as it landed on the concrete.

This was the sixth time he'd been on the trail since arriving yesterday. It was the only thing he could do. This and the gardens.

Ratchet had tried to explore the castle a few times. He wandered the hallways, moving from floor to floor. He wasn't able to go into all the rooms obviously, but he wanted to inspect the public areas. Every employee he crossed paths with eyed him suspiciously like he was up to something. They all thought it strange for him to be there when his room was so far away. A few even dared to ask him if he was lost and direct him away.

The trees were supposed to be haunted. Being on the trail after dark might be the ticket he needed for a show. A lot of people had gone missing out this way. The woods were dangerous by that reputation. They were packed with drop offs and wild animals. The trees were dense. It would be easy to become disoriented, lost. A person could die of thirst before finding their way out. With as many people who had rumored to die here, there had to be ghosts.

He began walking the trail and hadn't made it very far when he stopped for another shot of whisky. His head tilted back too fast when he lifted the bottle to his lips, and everything spun around him. He lost his balance and tried to catch himself before he fell. He overcorrected and landed on his back for the second time that night just off the trail.

The branches above him were circling. He couldn't stand up just yet. He felt like he was spinning and grabbed hold of the earth with both hands to stop himself from falling off the ground. He closed his eyes and waited a couple minutes for his body to right itself. When he opened them again, he felt better, clearer headed.

He stretched out his arm to grab one of the side rails of the walking path to help pull himself up, but couldn't reach. He had to roll over onto all fours and get up with the help of the trunk of a nearby tree. "Sorry," he said

Ratchet looked around and slowly began to panic. He didn't know where he was. All the trees blended together, and he wouldn't be able to tell one way from the next if it weren't for the trail. But, the trail was gone.

He felt hot and flushed. His breathing quickened, and he found himself slowly pushing his air out between his lips trying to regain control.

'No, it has to be here,' he told himself. *'It's just too dark to see.'*

There appeared to be a light a ways off in the distance. How he managed to stray that far from the path was beyond him, but he decided to walk in that direction hoping to find the trail. Each step was painstakingly careful, and he checked over his shoulder for the tree he woke up near. It was his only landmark.

He'd walked a little ways, and the light was diminishing as if he was walking away from it not toward it. The tree stayed behind him the whole time. One footstep sent earth crumbling, and he froze in place waiting for his eyes to adjust. There was a drop off. This wasn't the way to the trail.

Ratchet went back to the tree and considered what to do next. He could wait it out till morning, but the temperature had already dropped significantly. His whole body ached from the cold air, and he was starting to shiver. He'd be freezing before there was light to see by.

He walked away from the opposite side of the tree. He

hadn't made it very far when a shot rang out. He froze in place like his feet were stuck in tar. There were no other sounds, just a distant shot. Only it wasn't that far away. He couldn't see anything and wasn't sure if he should run or hide. *'Who else would be in these woods? And what are they shooting at?'*

"Just wait till I find you." The words were muttered, but Ratchet heard them clear enough. The footsteps of the other trespasser were near and growing closer.

It was enough to make him sprint. Ratchet didn't know who it was or what he was doing, but he wasn't going to stick around to find out either. He darted around trees and tried to avoid branches as best he could, but he could hear the other man gaining on him.

He'd ran far enough to make his chest ache. His body wasn't used to this type of exercise. The footsteps seemed to have stopped. He hid behind a tree and waited, listening, but the only sound he heard was the beating of his own heart echoing in his ears. When he felt like it might be safe, he peered around the tree.

A voice came from behind him. "That's enough," the man said. "We both know how this is going to end."

Ratchet turned to look at the man. There was nothing even vaguely familiar about him. Whoever he was looking for, it couldn't be him. It was just his luck he'd get lost in Ravenwood the same night a lunatic was on the prowl in the woods.

"What?" The man appeared just as shocked to see Ratchet. He took a couple steps back and studied him. The man sized him up from head to toe. The metal of the gun he was holding glinted in the light from the night sky falling through the branches of the trees.

Ratchet held his breath hoping the man would realize his mistake. Even then, there was no guarantee he'd just walk away.

The man cocked the gun and aimed it at Ratchet. "On your knees."

He raised his arms, but looked around for an exit. There was nowhere to run the bullet couldn't find him.

"Your knees!" The man shouted at him when he didn't comply.

Ratchet dropped to the ground and shook with fear as the man slowly approached him. All he could do now was hope there'd be answers. Somehow his body would be found, and his wife would know it wasn't only his stupidity driving him into the woods which caused his death. Foul play was involved as well.

The man lifted the gun a little higher and pointed it directly at his head. He was standing in a direct beam of moonlight, and it was the only thing in the woods Ratchet could see clearly. Ratchet's eyes widened when he saw it, but the man didn't seem affected. Not at first.

A branch – it was brown and too thick to be a vine – wrapped itself around the man's ankle and climbed up his leg. It made it almost to the man's waist when he finally took notice. He reached for it and stumbled back a step, but the branch had picked up speed and had locked him in place.

The branch wrapped around the man's back and shot through his chest. The man lurched forward, coughing, and looking down at the foreign object sticking out of him with widened, dazed eyes. He couldn't move away or fall. The branch was holding him in place and continued to circle him.

A different branch, or an off shoot of the same one,

traveled down the man's arm to his hand. The gun fired, and Ratchet fell to the ground on his stomach. His head was turned to the side and he peaked under closed eyelids to watch. A piece of the branch was shot off and fell to the ground. Ratchet heard it cry out in pain.

Another branch entered the man's mouth, down his throat, suffocating the man. Within seconds, the man was completely encased in branches. It looked like a tree grew around him. When it was over, there was a tree trunk in the man's place with an outstretched branch that appeared to be holding a wooden gun. In place of the man's face was a giant knot hole, staring at him in terror.

Several men walked out of the woods, and Ratchet screamed. The trees began to spin, and he passed out before they could identify themselves as police officers.

More by Jennifer Lush

Available in eBook, Paperback, and Kindle Vella

The Elementals Series

Air

Earth

Fire

Water

Balance

Ravenwood: Volume One

The Below: Phillipe's Revenge

The Below: Mezzie's Prison

Fogpoint Harbor

The Inheritance

Buried Secrets

The Sacrificial Dagger

About the Author

Jennifer Lush is a mother of three from central Illinois where she has lived her entire life. Aside from spending time with her children and grandchildren, writing and traveling are her two main consuming passions. Luckily, they are mutually beneficial.

Writing has always been in her blood even if it took her longer than planned to do it. One of her earliest memories of longing to be an author happened in kindergarten when she told her parents what she wanted to be when she grew up. It took close to four decades, but she has finally made that childhood dream come true.

Jennifer is an entertainer at heart who is always making those around her laugh. She can turn any mundane event into a story worth repeating with flair. Inspiration for her fictional worlds comes from everywhere. There are more ideas floating through her mind than she has time to write, but she is determined to finish as many as possible.

Twitter: AuthorJLush
IG: AuthorJenniferLush
Tik Tok: AuthorJenniferLush

www.ingramcontent.com/pod-product-compliance
Lightning Source LLC
Chambersburg PA
CBHW020802190726
48285CB00006B/2136